Seasons of Forgiveness
A Collection of Short Stories

Dale Heinold

Dedicated to my darling wife Betty and her love of story.

CONTENTS

Introduction

On these pages are short stories written over the span of nearly twenty years. Some such as The Nurses Hat and Danny's Firetruck are from that first set of stories written so long ago. Others such as Five Smooth Stones and Dewey Springs are the most recent.

The stories themselves bear one unintended commonality – the power and need of forgiveness. Many, if not most, have a Christian frame of reference since that is my view of the world. Not that forgiveness is only possible within that framework, but in my experience, it is the seat of complete forgiveness and healing.

Also, in these pages you'll discover five seasons. The fifth being the Christmas season with the angel's declaration of peace on earth and Christ's mission of forgiveness.

Blessings,

Dale Heinold (July 2019)

Seasons of Forgiveness: Spring

FIVE SMOOTH STONES

One day a man sat beside a lovely tree-lined rocky stream -- the kind of place one could sit for hours soaking in peace as the flowing water carried off your worry and stress.

Sitting there that day, the man thought of his troubled world. To him, it all seemed like a mighty giant, a Goliath, filled with rage impossible to overcome. One by one, the man thought of the troubles, the struggles, the injustice, and the darkness. He searched them hoping to discover an exploitable weakness but ultimately gave up.

As the man sat with bowed head, the tears rolling down his cheeks falling into the stream. "Thanks for this moment," he said with a sigh to the creator of the stream as the last teardrop fell. At that moment the air stirred, trees rustled their leaves, and a sparkle of light caught his eye as it bounced from a nearby stone.

The flat, rounded, and plain stone was nothing special. It had neither the speckles of granite or the stripes of sandstone. The man picked up the stone. It fit well in his hand like an old silver dollar. "Change the world with love," the wind whispered.

A few paces downstream, the man found another stone like the first. "Change the world with forgiveness," the wind whispered as he picked it up. Three more times the man discovered the sisters and brothers of the plain stone. Each with a word whispered on the wind.

The man sat again beside the stream. "Is that it?" He questioned trying to imagine how these five smooth stones could change the world. Could these words defeat the troubles, struggles, injustice, violence, and darkness of his world?

With a shrug, the man left the tree-lined stream with his collection of five smooth stones.

Once home, and with great care, the man painted the stones. Emblazoning each with one of the five words. But he puzzled over what to do next. A mystery solved when he took out the trash for the weekly pickup.

Strewn across his lawn was everything from his neighbor's trash can. Used paper towels, spent soda cans, various plastic wrappers, even a couple of dirty diapers speckled his yard. His first thought was to march over to the neighbor and demand that he fix it. "It's his trash, not mine," he thought as he thrust his hands in his pockets. But when his fingers felt the stones, he stopped.

Pulling out one of the stones he read, "change the world with forgiveness." Slowly, one piece at a time, he began collecting the used paper towels, dirty diapers, and the other trash. About half-way through his efforts, the neighbor, leaving for the market, saw the mess. "Hey man,

I'm sorry," the neighbor said as he helped with the cleanup effort.

"It can happen to any of us," the man replied. "Umm, here I have something for you," the man said as he passed the forgiveness stone to the neighbor.

"What do I do with this?" the neighbor asked.

"I know it sounds silly, but when you get a chance, give it to someone else who needs forgiveness," the man replied. The neighbor didn't say anything but simply pocketed the stone and walked away.

The next day the man had another opportunity. A co-worker misunderstood an email the man had sent, twisting the meaning in ways never intended. After a flurry of messages, the man offered to meet to the co-worker over lunch to "hash things out."

Their conversation was tense at first, but the man determined to follow one of the stones. So, he listened, expressed his feelings, and listened some more. While difficulties remained, the man felt he understood his co-worker concern.

As they were leaving the table, the man reached in his pocket. "Hey, can I give you something?" the man asked his co-worker.

"Sure, I guess," the co-worker replied.

The man handed the co-worker a stone painted "change the world with understanding." And said, "just pass it on when you get a chance."

That evening he gave away the stone marked "change the world with kindness" after helping a mother of three load groceries into her car. A few days later, he gave away "change the world with hope" as he visited a neighbor recovering from knee surgery.

The man knew that the hardest stoner remained. "It's easy to say love, but how do you do love?" the man pondered. He recognized that the previous four stones had aspects of love so this last stone had to be a special kind of love. "In its own time," the man concluded.

Several weeks later the man was standing in the checkout line at the local Super-Mart. In front of him was a low-income family with two loaded shopping carts. Behind him was an impatient young man with a scraggly beard and some auto parts. "Bet they're on food stamps," the young man said loud enough for the family to hear.

The man turned, "So?"

"They should get out of our way, go back to jungle or wherever they came from," he said even louder.

"That's not necessary, they belong here as much as you do," the man said.

The young man responded with a torrent of darkness which the man tried to push back. "Enough!" the man shouted.

"You got that right," the young man said, throwing a bottle jack at the man's head before running out of the store.

The heavy bottle jack glanced off the side the man's head knocking him out. The stone painted "Change the world with love" fell from his pocket and slid across the floor to the feet of the family's father.

It took several days of worry and prayer before the man opened his eyes again. "Am I alive?" he rasped.

"You sure are Mr. Brown. You're in the hospital with a head injury," a nurse replied.

"I guess Goliath got the best of me," he whispered.

"I wouldn't say that. Can you see over to the counter?" the nurse asked.

"Sure, why all the buckets?" he asked. "Got a leaky roof?"

The nurse walked over and picked a painted stone from one of the buckets. "These started coming in soon after you got here. The news interviewed the father of the family you stood up for. He showed them the stone that fell from your pocket. They also interviewed others with similar stories, and these began to show up. Hundreds of them. All painted with "change the world with love, kindness, forgiveness, hope, or understanding."

The man laid his head back down as tears of joy streaked his cheeks.

CHASING SUNSETS

It was a late spring day, and the garden needed some fence wire to tame an over-exuberant blackberry vine. The wire happened to be in the barn.

I don't go out to the old barn very often. The animals are all gone now, and cousin Ronnie is farming our ground. My wife Dot and I still live on the home place but not for much longer. I was born on this plot of ground in the middle of Illinois and raised my children here. Our barn is close to 100 years old, and it's one of my favorite places. The ground level livestock area has given shelter to every kind of farm animal you can think of. The stalls are all clean now, the only residents being a few cats and some stubborn mice.

Upstairs is the hayloft. Nothing smells like summer more than drying hay. It's hard to describe. There's a sweetness in the breeze that recalls hard work and satisfaction as the hay is baled and lifted into the loft for winter feeding. When we fed cattle, the hayloft would be completely filled with straw and hay by the first snow.

Now, the few bales left are slowly turning to dust as time passes.

I swung open the top of the dutch door and reach in to unhook the bottom. Memory reminds me there's a roll of wire hanging on a nail just past the ladder to the loft. I brushed away a few cobwebs and spied a mouse seeking shelter from the light pouring in the open door. The wire was right where I thought.

I considered taking a detour up to the hayloft. Relaxing on the haystack is one of my favorite places to get away from things. A quiet space to put things in perspective or work through a knotty problem. There is something about the sweet dryness that makes it ok to let go. I took a deep breath, hoping to catch a whiff of long-ago summers. But there was something else, something that smelled like scorched straw. Fire? Couldn't be but I had to check it out.

I used to scamper up the ladder, but now it's a long trip, one painful step at a time. Finally, I poked my head through and looked up at the oak-beamed roof. Sure enough, there was a tiny wisp of smoke hanging in the air. The threat of fire motivated me to scamper up the final rungs.

In one corner someone was leaning over a makeshift burner heating a pot that I assumed was water. The tin can burner rested on a brick. My uninvited visitor concentrated on feeding it straw to keep the fire going.

"Hello?" I say as if meeting someone on the street so as not to startle them. I can't risk them upsetting the tin can stove.

The visitor looks up and sighs. Seemed she was

hoping to avoid being found. "Could you put out the fire, I really don't want to lose my barn today." With another sigh, she lifted the pot of water and poured it down the stove. "Thanks," I said.

Now that the fire is out, I can see that she is a 40ish hiker. A new backpack leans against a straw bale. Some hiking poles rest against the wall. Her outfit is simple and practical, white t-shirt and Capri style walking shorts. A few strands of raven black hair escape from under a Chicago Cubs ball cap while laugh lines dog her eyes.

She wasn't the first unexpected visitor this old barn had seen. When I was a kid at the tail end of the depression, hobos would often stop by to spend the night. These men would travel the Nickel Plate rails chasing rumors of jobs. Mom would feed them and dad would fix up a place for them to rest in the hayloft. Dad always asked them the same question.

"Walking to something or from something?" I asked, like dad.

"I'm walking Route 66," she replied.

I nod my head. Walking from something it seemed. Folks going somewhere tend to share they're plans and desires with gusto. Those walking from something, not so much. "That's quite the hike, what about 2000 miles?"

"2400 from Chicago to Santa Monica Pier," she replied. "I started out a week ago. I thought I had trained right, but my feet are killing me. I was hoping to give them a rest for a day or two, but I'll clean up and get out of your way."

I walked over and extended my hand, "I'm Bill, Bill Haines."

"Cassidy Baxter, call me Cass," she replied, shaking my hand. "Sorry, I, um, didn't ask permission."

"Bygones are bygones, let's get you to the house. We have a spare room and Dot can tend to your feet."

"I don't want to be any trouble." she pushed back.

"And I'd rather you didn't set fire to my barn. We'll call it an even trade." Cass collected her things and winced as she pulls on her hiking boots. While she was packing, I gave the area a close inspection for any stray embers that could flare into something worse.

    ***

Dot's eyes betrayed her wonder. I had left to get some wire and came back with someone old enough to be our daughter. But it didn't take her long to size up the situation, gather up her gardening tools, and head inside. By the time Cass and I hobbled back from the barn, Dot had drawn a pan of warm water and added a healthy dose of Epsom salts.

"Dot meet Cass, she's walking Route 66 to California." Dot and Cass shake hands. What a contrast. Dot's white curls to Cass's short straight black locks, Dot's farmer's wife dress to Cass's hiking gear. Dare I mention Dot's rather plump figure compared to Cass's lean frame? I guess I already did.

"Sit here honey and soak your feet in that pan, it will bring down the swelling." Dot suggested with a smile.

"And let me see those boots. I did a fair amount of walking in the army." I offered.

"AAhhh," was all Cass offered as her feet hit the water and she relaxed back in the chair.

While Cass soaked, Dot threw together some sandwiches for lunch while I took a closer look at Cass's boots. They were fancier than anything I had in the army. Her boots seemed more suited for day hikes at Starved Rock, not a 2400 mile trip on hard roads. My farm boots come from Wilson's. A long-established shoe store not far from downtown Peoria. Since they may have what she needs, I give them a call and explain the situation.

After a bit, Cass sits up, "Oh, that feels better, thanks."

"Here's a towel dear, dry your feet and come to the table. Lunch is ready. It's not much, only some sandwiches and chips." Dot offered.

I wasn't sure how our guest would react to this next part. Dot and I always pause to hold hands and say grace before our meals. So I took one of Dot's hands and we each offered a hand to Cass. "We're going to say grace," I explained. She nods and tentatively takes hold. Compared to her soft hands, ours must have felt like sandpaper paws. "Thank you, Lord, for this food and for bringing Cass our way. Heal her feet and bring blessings to our day. We love you, Jesus – Amen."

"So Cass, what made you decide to tackle Route 66?" I asked, handing her the sandwich plate.

"Seemed like the thing to do," she shrugged. "What kind of meat is this, Salami of some kind?"

"It's Lebanon bologna from Pennsylvania. We have some friends out there. They send us some every now and again while we send them apple cider donuts and other goodies from a local orchard."

"It's great, somewhere between summer sausage and

smoked salami," Cass observed.

"While you were soaking I called Wilson's, it's a shoe place in Peoria down on Adams. Been there forever. They think they may have a better hiking boot for you. To be honest, the boots you have are made for day hikes, not the road. We can head in after lunch If you'd like."

Before Cass could answer Dot added, "And you're welcome to stay for supper and spend the night. We have a guest room; you're more than welcome to use it."

***

During the trip to Peoria, I tried cracking Cass's shell to learn more about her reasons for choosing her long hike. Instead, I found out that she's very adept at deflecting. For instance, I asked when she thought she would arrive in Santa Monica, she replied with a question about corn. Definitely walking from something.

Wilson's did have the boots she needed. Turns out that the clerk had completed the Appalachian Trail a few years ago and gave Cass some pointers. The owner even offered to sponsor Cass's trek and provide her boots at a discount. During those conversations, I learned that Cass launched without any support system to back her up.

On the trip back from Peoria, I decided to take the blunt route with Cass. "You don't have anyone, do you? No family or friends to backstop you?" A little quiver of her lower lip and a vacant stare out the window confirmed my suspicions. "We haven't known each other very long, but Dot and I are willing to support you."

"My name is Cassidy Baxter," Cass began in a dry

monotone as her vacant gaze stared at the road ahead. "As of three months ago, I was Cassidy Morgan. Married twenty-four years with no children. Vice-President of marketing at Chicago Trust and Savings. I'm 49 years old. My husband took his mid-life crisis to the ultimate extreme. He traded in his car, his career, and his wife for newer models. One month ago they passed me over for a promotion which should have been mine. I worked for it, slaved for it, gave up a family for it. I resigned the next day without notice. That bridge is well burnt, including connections to my coworkers. I thought some of them were my friends, but only the job held us together. I have no other family, only a second cousin in Florida that I don't know and don't care to know. All I'm doing is chasing sunsets until I die." She said with flowing tears.

Ok, that shell is thoroughly shattered, and it was more than I bargained for. "Well, let me return that favor. I'm William Haines, 78 years old. Dorothy, Dot, and I have been married for fifty-eight years. We have three grown children scattered hither and yon with seven grandchildren and two great-grandchildren. All which bring us enormous joy and pride. We're old and retired but in relatively ok health. Soon, we'll have to give up living on the home place which makes me very sad. Our friends are dying off, so there's that. But we have our faith and we have each other, our family, and a few close friends so as far as I'm concerned life is good."

The last few miles were silent as we both pondered those words.

***

15

Cassidy stayed more than overnight. The clerk at Wilson's had suggested a series of short hikes to break in her new boots before she set off again in earnest. Dot and I didn't mind, it was a joy to have someone else share our lives.

Over the next few evenings, Cass and I planned her journey. One evening we cut her route out of a road atlas. The next day, while Cass hiked to a neighboring town and back, I ran to the local school to laminate the pieces.

Another evening we looked at her pack. "Try that pack on, I want to see how it fits you," I said. Cass shoulders the pack and sets the hip belt. "It's riding a bit much on your shoulders. You want most of the weight to hit your hips. Let's see if we can't adjust that." I helped Cass out of the pack. "How much stuff do you have in there? I've thrown 50lb feed sacks that seemed lighter."

"It's everything I need." Cass shrugged.

"Mind if we go through it? Shaving a few pounds will be easier on your feet," I suggested.

She struggled with the thought for a moment. It's difficult to let someone else look into our lives and suggest things we don't need. Trust won over fear, thank God for small victories. Within a few moments, everything is out on the kitchen table.

I won't go through her inventory. Let's only say that she was able to throw away some things and arranged for us to send other things when needed. In all, we shaved ten pounds by the time we finished. We spent the rest of the evening planning where and when to send her the care packages.

The next day at breakfast, Cass announced, "I'm ready to start again. I'll hike about twenty miles today and I'd like to fix supper for you tonight as a way of saying thanks. Then I'll head out early tomorrow morning."

"That would be lovely dear, feel free to use whatever you need in the kitchen." Dot replied.

"Oh no, I'm doing this hiking style, any chance you could set up a fire ring somewhere? I'll take care of everything else, even the firewood. The only thing I need is a fire ring, I'll pick everything else up at the store."

Later, the three of us contentedly sat around Cass's campfire as the sun's rim kissed the western horizon. Cass's foil pack creation of bratwurst, onions, green peppers, and potatoes hit the spot. Clean up was quick and a fire built up from the charcoal embers.

"Going to be a pretty one," I said, looking at the western sky. Orange was prominent, but I knew that as the sun dipped lower the clouds would soon glow with purples and reds.

"We haven't done this in years, I kind of miss our campfires," Dot said snuggling closer.

"I don't know how to thank you two, I never expected, even dreamed, that folks would care," Cass admitted.

"Ah, it was nothing if it kept you from setting fire to the barn," I joked.

"You asked a question that morning," Cass began. "You know, about walking from something or to something. To be honest, I didn't know how to answer. All my life, I've walked to something only to see it fall apart or out of my grasp. So, yeah, I am walking away from a lot of somethings, a truckload of pain, heartache, and regrets. Truth is that I'd like to walk towards something, I don't know what though."

"I guess you'll have 2400 miles to figure that out," I said. Cass stared at the fire and nodded as the reds faded from the clouds and dusk took hold.

"You're carrying a terrible burden dear," Dot said.

"It's a lot less thanks to Bill," she replied.

"Oh, I don't mean your backpack. I mean in your heart." Dot paused to let the words settle.

"Yeah, I know," Cass whispered. "I don't know how to change that. It's not like sorting a pack and throwing things away."

"Well, its kind of is like that," I replied. "I carried a load like that myself for a while."

"Go on dear, tell Cass about it." Dot encouraged knowing my reluctance to revisit old wounds.

"Well, you know I was in the army. It was during the Korean War. I wasn't infantry, but in communications, mostly rear lines stuff. Setting up phones, running messages, and delivering orders. Pretty tame compared to what a lot of the boys went through. One morning they ordered me to deliver a message to a platoon on some numbered hill. We'd run phone up there several times, but the lines kept getting sabotaged.

So I drove there in a Jeep with a few replacements. It was an uneventful trip, but by the time we got there, it was too late to head back. The Chinese attacked that night, but we were in a strong defensive position. The captain had me radio in for some artillery support. Someone in the chain between my lips and the gunner's ears transposed a number. The army never figured out who. But that error caused the artillery shells to fall on us instead of the Chinese. Luckily we managed to get a radio call out but not before half the platoon was killed or injured. I ended up with two broken legs and a trip stateside for the rest of the war."

"How long did it take to recover?" Cass asked.

"Little over a year physically, but heart-wise? Well, that took a lot longer. I was mad at everyone. Mad at the Sargent that sent me up there, the Captain that ordered the artillery, the dunderhead that transposed the numbers, the gunner that failed to double-check the map, the Army, the government, the Koreans, but most of all God for letting it happen."

"Yep, I've got a list like that too," Cass agreed. "So how did you deal with it?"

"Even though I was mad at God, I still went to church for the kid's sake. One day the preacher talked about what Jesus told us to pray – forgive our debts as we forgive our debtors. I guess I kind of took that to heart. Farming is a lonely business, kind of like walking Route 66 solo. Hours and hours out on the tractor working the fields. So I began to forgive everyone and everything I could think of as I worked the ground. It was like little chips of heaviness fell off with every word until there wasn't anything left."

"I watched it happen dear and I prayed that God would keep showing him things to get rid of." Dot added.

"I don't want to fool you, it wasn't easy or quick. Several times I thought I had it all gone, but God would show me a little bit more. Soon though, I was going beyond what happened in Korea and forgiving things that happened earlier in my life or even that same day."

Cass nodded but didn't say anything, choosing instead to soak in the silence of the stars, the crackling warmth of the fire, and the distant call of a coyote. I don't know if Cass caught it, but my ears heard a whisper on the breeze saying, "it is well."

***

Several months later an email landed in our inbox. The subject line said, "Thanks." The body of the email had one line, "I feel a thousand tons lighter." Attached was a picture of Cass standing in the ocean with a mile-wide grin as the sunset splashed on Santa Monica Pier.

"She made it!" I yelled to Dot.

"Praise God," she replied.

THE FAMILY RULES

Bob's Foot-Stompin Barbeque is the place to be. Or at least it seems that way given the overflowing lunchtime parking lot and the buzz of the dining room. Being near the busy Branson strip, Bob's customers come from many backgrounds. So far I've been able to pick out the locals, the sophisticates fresh from a round of golf, the shoppers taking a break from the local craft and outlet malls. There are tables of work buddies, young families, older couples, and a few generational tables. Our table may be unique, however, since we're a honeymoon table.

Debbie and I said our wedding vows a few days ago. And sure, there are other trendier places for a honeymoon. But when you barely have two nickels to rub together and your aunt gives you a free week in her time-share condo, well it beats a weekend at the Motel Eight by a country mile.

Around Bob's tables, memories are created over plates of ribs and pulled pork. Plans made for the next show, the next adventure, the next round of shopping. It's in that noisy, busy, wonderful place where I meet Frank.

Frank is an old determined soul. I watch as he inches across the parking lot with a cane in each hand. His wife, evidently knowing that Frank is ok walks ahead and waits in the shade by the door. Once inside, they search for a place to land and wander to some tables near us. Anticipating a larger group, they struggle to pull tables together.

"May I help?" I ask.

"Would you please," the white-haired woman answers. "We need enough space for seven." I help them push a couple of tables together and set some chairs.

"So where are you from?" I ask. Not the most original question but without doubt the most common one in the touristy town.

"We're from Little Rock. I'm Frank, by the way, thanks for helping out," the older man says.

"We're from Illinois, near Peoria. I'm Daniel. Are you meeting up with your family?" I ask.

"Yep, four generations all told," Frank answers with a smile.

"It's only the two of us," I replied, pointing at our nearby table.

Debbie and I soon gathered up our leftovers and leave Bob's foot-stompin Barbeque. That was the last time I expected to meet Frank, but it wasn't.

The next evening we decide to take in Presley's Country Jubilee Show. Well, we didn't decide, it was another gift. The Presley's show is a blend of country music and comedy that has entertained audiences for over fifty years. And yes, they are shirt-tail cousins to the best know Presley of all time. During intermission, the emcee calls out the birthdays and anniversaries in the audience while a video camera shows them on the big screens flanking the stage. The emcee calls out another name I don't recognize and congratulates them for their 65th wedding anniversary. I look up at the big screen, and there are Frank and his wife sitting across the auditorium.

I pop out of my seat and work my way toward them. "Hi, remember me? Congratulations," I said once I arrive at their seats.

Frank looks up, "Peoria, right? Bob's Barbeque? What was it? Dale?"

"Daniel," I reply with a laugh. "Sixty-five years, so what's the secret?"

"I keep her locked in the fruit cellar and only let her out for holidays and vacations," he replies with a twinkle.

"You're so ornery, now behave," Frank's wife says, poking him with her elbow.

"I'm sorry ma'am, I never caught your name."

"Maribelle, but most folks call me Belle."

"Nice to meet you, Belle," I say, shaking her hand.

"So, Belle, what is the secret for staying married sixty-five years?"

"Ladies and Gentlemen, please take your seat. The second half of the Presley's Country Jubilee is about to begin." The announcer calls out, ending our conversation.

There are some people you meet which are soon forgotten. Chance encounters you don't expect to be repeated. But there are some like Frank and Belle that seem to take a life of their own. I lost them in the crowd after the show and figured that was that. But it wasn't.

Along the Branson strip are many restaurants. Some

are well-known chains, while a few are local favorites. Several of them have live entertainment. One of those places is the Hard Luck Cafe. A hamburger and shake joint with a 50's look that hires wait staff hoping for their break into show business. One moment your waitress is taking your order the next moment she's singing with a microphone in hand.

We decide to take a break from shopping and hit the Hard Luck for lunch. As the hostess leads us to our booth, a cane shoots out and I almost have 15 seconds of embarrassing fame. It's Frank and Belle.

"Well that's one way of getting a guy's attention," I said seeing the twinkle in Frank's eye. "Nice to see you again."

"Why don't you sit with us? We just got here too, and I still owe you an answer," Frank suggests.

Debbie and I exchanged quick glances. I'm still learning to read her face, so I think she's ok with this. "Sure," I reply and convey our desire to the hostess. "Frank, Belle, this is my wife Debbie," I say by way of introductions as we slide into the red leather booth.

"How long have you two been married?" Belle asks.

"Three and a half days," Debbie answers, hugging my arm. "How about you two?"

"Celebrating our Sixty-Fifth," Frank begins.

"Wait," Belle interrupts, "Were you married on the fourteenth?" We both nod. "That's our day too," Belle says with a chuckle. "Who would have thought."

"We were hoping to run into you again," Frank begins once our orders are in. "Truth is I wasn't sure how to answer your question about staying married. Never thought much about it."

"Frank and I have been talking and thinking about it ever since Presley's," Belle adds.

"We had two basic rules when we got married, never mention divorce and never go to bed angry. And those are good but don't come close to covering all the things we've done or learned along the way," Frank continues.

"So yesterday as we slowly wandered around a craft store," Belle says.

"It's the only speed I've got," Frank adds.

"And we found this sign that pretty much says it all. I know you're not supposed to, but I snuck a picture of it," Belle whispers handing me her phone as if it held state secrets. "Family Rules," the rustic sign in the picture announces. "Be kind, love one another, laugh together, do your chores, tell the truth, say your prayers, be forgiving, celebrate life, encourage each other, be respectful, share blessings, have fun, live well."

"I like it," I reply and hand the phone to Debbie.

"Mind you, we haven't been perfect in these things," Frank said. "But that sums it up better than anything we could come up with on my own."

Between songs, hamburgers, fries, and shakes, we get to know more about Frank and Belle. He's a retired factory worker and she's a retired school teacher. They have three children, two of whom are in Branson with them. And so far they have seven grandchildren and two great-grandchildren. But more than learning their surface history I watch as they interact. How they tease each other, correct each other, and love each other.

"Say, could you tell me where that craft mall is at? The one with the sign?" I ask as we get ready to leave.

"Let's see. It's on the yellow route just past the winery. Julie's, I think," Belle said.

"Judy's, its Judy's Craft Mall, a little south of the winery," Frank corrected.

"Thanks," Debbie replied. "I know where that is."

And that is the last we saw of Frank and Belle. Later that afternoon, we find Judy's Craft Mall and the sign about family rules. It stretches our budget a bit, but we decide to get it anyway.

"Kind of crazy running into them so many times," Debbie says as we walk out to the car.

"Yeah, but I'm glad we did," I reply. Carefully placing the sign in the back seat.

"What do you think, come back to Branson in sixty-five years?" Debbie asks.

"Well, we can come back sooner than that, right?"

"Sure, if you want too," she replies.

"Well, whether it's Branson or somewhere else I hope and pray that in sixty-five years, we're just like Frank and Belle."

"Amen to that," she says, reaching for my hand.

THE BLACKROCK CHALLENGE

Jeremy was caught. For months he had snuck around the village stealing valuables and causing mischief. His latest misadventure involved stealing the Elder's cherry pie as it cooled on the window sill. Not as profitable as his earlier thefts but infinitely more challenging and pleasing. That is until he was caught eating the stolen pie under Mrs. McGuffin's porch. That one mistake revealed much.

The Elder convened a council and instructed the constable to search Jeremy's home. What they found astonished them. All the treasures, the coins, the jewelry, the toys, he had stolen were discovered and brought before the council. For example, Mr. Harmon identified his favorite hammer. Mrs. Brecth an heirloom pearl necklace. Jeremy's haul touched every home of the village.

"Young man, do you have any words to defend yourself?" The Elder boomed.

"Well...I... no sir," Jeremy replied.

"You are right. There is no defense, no plausible explanation or reason why we should forgive you. You did not steal out of want or hunger. It would seem that you only stole these items to please yourself," The folks of the village murmured their approval of the Elder's words. The Elder solemnly rose and struck the Bell of Decision three times to pronounce Jeremy's punishment. "It is the will of this council to sentence you, Jeremy Wilkins, to complete the Blackrock Challenge as punishment for your crimes." A collective gasp escaped from the crowd at the sentence.

"Tomorrow at dawn," the Elder continued, "You will be taken to the Wasteland Gate. You will have three days to travel the wasteland, find Blackrock mound, and return to the gate with proof. You may take nothing for your journey except the robe of shame." The Elder struck the bell once, ending the council.

"No, no, no," Jeremy muttered and sank to his knees.

"It's a death sentence," Mrs. Bretch whispered retrieving her pearls.

"No one has ever completed the challenge," another responded retrieving a treasured book from the table.

"But he's guilty, he must be punished," declared Mr. Harmon as he retrieved his hammer.

An older man bent with age slowly approached the table to collect a pewter mug that once belonged to his great grandfather. "Yes, Jeremy is guilty. That fact is true," he said. "But, well, something just seems wrong about all of this."

"O, come now, Joshua. He's a thief many times over and getting what he deserves." Mr. Harmon shot back.

"No doubt, no doubt," Joshua softly agreed as he left the crowd around the table.

--

Neither Jeremy or Joshua slept well that night. Jeremy out of dread of the Blackrock Challenge. Every time he did find sleep, his dreams were invaded with one of the many ways he could die in the wasteland.

Joshua struggled with other demons. Why throw away a life over such trinkets he kept thinking. Around midnight he gave up, put a match to the lamp, and retrieved the bylaws of the Village. "Perhaps this will put me to sleep," he muttered.

Before dawn, the Elder, Constable, Jeremy, and a few hearty souls gathered at the Wasteland Gate. Slow to approach was Joshua. Once the sun peaked over the eastern mountains, the Elder nodded.

The Constable unlocked the gate and unshackled Jeremy, who was already wearing the coarse robe. "Jeremy Wilkins, do you understand the rules of the challenge?"

"Sure, I die," Jeremy muttered.

"Does anyone have any last-minute words which would change this sentence," the Elder announced per the bylaws of the Village.

"Yes," Joshua softly said, "Yes, I do."

Surprised, the Elder answered, "Speak then."

"I declare the right of redemption," Joshua firmly said.

"You what!" the Elder chocked. "No one has claimed that right in over a hundred years, and never for this. Are you sure old man?"

"I claim the right of redemption," Joshua repeated.

"I will take Jeremy's place and his punishment. You cannot refuse me, it is in the book."

There was murmuring and bluster as the news rustled through the small crowd and out to every home and hovel of the village.

"Look, I appreciate the thought, but you can't do this. I'm guilty..." Jeremy began.

"I declare the right of redemption. This is my call and I will not change my mind," Joshua declared.

Seeing that the path was set the Elder ordered the constable to take Jeremy and Joshua into a nearby home to exchange the robe of shame and prepare Joshua for the challenge.

Standing before the unlocked gate, Joshua heard the Elder's final pronouncement. "Joshua Higgins, since you have declared the right of redemption you will endure Jeremy's sentence. You have three days to wander the wasteland, find Blackrock mound, and return with proof of our journey. You may take nothing save the robe of shame. As a gift of mercy, you may also take your staff because of your age."

The gate mourned as the constable pulled it open. A blast of hot, dusty air flew through the open gate. Jeremy fell to his knees and watched as Joshua walked through the gate without looking back. The Constable forced the gate closed while everyone began drifting home. All except Jeremy.

For the first few hours, Jeremy said nothing but only wept as he knelt against the Wasteland Gate. At noon the Elder came by after hearing the murmurs in the village about Jeremy. "Go home, Jeremy, it is over," He said.

"Why did you let him go?" Jeremy asked, with tears rolling down his cheeks. "He didn't deserve to die."

"I had no choice, he declared the right of redemption. The right to take your place so that you could live." the Elder answered.

"Why did he do it? What am I to him?" Jeremy pleaded.

"That I cannot answer, no one can look with clarity into another's heart. But it doesn't matter. The deed is done. You're free, go home."

"I can't, I have to see it through until the third day," Jeremy said with the hint of resolve.

"Well if you must stay then take this," the Elder said, offering a wrapped piece of bread.

"No, he's out there with no food or water struggling against the dry dust of the wasteland. Neither will I eat or drink until he returns or the three days expire." Jeremy said with greater resolve.

The Elder shook his head at Jeremy as if to say "stupid child" and walked away. But the questions still gnawed at Jeremy. Why did Joshua take his place? What had he done to deserve it or earn it? Questions he couldn't answer.

Throughout the day, Jeremy sat in the dust with his back against the gate. Those who passed heard him muttering over and over again, "why?" Those few who took pity by offering a cup of water or a bit of food were denied. But to all that offered, he asked if they knew why Joshua took his place.

At the time of the evening meal, Mrs. Brecth, from whom Jeremy had stolen a pearl necklace, came to the gate.

"I'm going to miss that old fool," she mutters.

Jeremy lifted his head towards Mrs. Brecht. "Why did he do it? Why did he take my place? Please tell me," he pleaded.

Mrs. Bretch face softened, "I suppose he saw something in you that shouldn't be thrown away. He has always seen things in ways others don't."

A strong silence enveloped them as Jeremy pondered her insight. "I'm sorry I stole your necklace. Is there something, anything, I can do to make it up to you? Yard work, fixing something, anything?"

"Perhaps that old fool is right. Yes, I think there is something you could do. Come around tomorrow after the first meal."

"I'll be there," Jeremy said with a smile of relief.

The next morning Jeremy went to Mrs. Brecht's and fixed a hole in her roof. All that day, Jeremy sought those he had wronged asking them if there were any odd jobs he could do for them. By the close of the second day of Joshua's Blackrock Challenge, he had mended a fence, hung some pictures, painted a door, and weeded a garden. In the evening he returned to the gate and resumed his vigil.

For the entire third day, Jeremy remained at the gate hoping to hear the knock of Joshua's return but also fearing the worse. As the day wore on, others joined the vigil. Each brought a little something, a bit of food, a little water, some clothes, all in hopes of Joshua's return. By the time of the evening meal, the whole village was at the gate.

As the rim of the sun touched the western mountains, the villagers quietly listened. Hoping to hear Joshua's knock. But hope faded with each moment. When the sun disappeared behind the distant range, the Elder solemnly declared "The challenge is over" and walked away from the gate. The murmur and buzz of the crowd grew as they all gathered themselves to go home. But Jeremy, seated with his back against the gate, felt something.

"Could it be?" he whispered. He pressed his ear to the wooden gate and heard a faint tap. "Quiet!" He yelled. In the silence, all heard three weak taps.

Seasons of Forgiveness: Summer

A TATTOOED HEART

I'm an artist whether you like it or not. My brushes are needles and my canvas is skin. You can call me Red or don't call me anything at all, I don't care. Or at least I didn't know until a few weeks ago.

Most folks want their skin art to say something, to mean something. Sometimes rebellious, sometimes tribal, occasionally cute, and yes, sometimes stupid. They think that a band of barbed wire around their biceps makes them strong. Or a flower makes them attractive. The worst, of course, is the Chinese characters that don't mean anything close to what they think it does. But hey, who am I to judge. Sign the papers, pay the money, and I'll ink you with whatever, well almost whatever, you want.

A few weeks ago I was finishing up an ankle rose for a "don't tell my mommy" but old enough to sign blond chick when he came in. I'd inked his arms a few times in the past. Nice work even if I do say so myself. "I want this across my back, can you get it done in three weeks?" He says unrolling a sheet of tracing paper. The design was intricate and large, monochrome with lots of shading.

"Three weeks is pushing it," I replied. "Turn around a moment." Holding the drawing against his back, I mumbled, "I'll have the scale it down and make several templates." Setting the drawing down, I asked him to turn back around. "It's going to take a lot of sessions, will be expensive, and hurt like hell, but yeah, I can do it." We arrive at a price and agree to start tomorrow.

Sometimes I can understand why someone wants a certain image. Sometimes I don't. One time, a farmer boy from the sticks wanted some Chinese-looking characters for his arm. He swore up and down meant powerful dragon, they didn't, and I couldn't talk him out of it. So now he'll spend the rest of his life with "bird fart" inked into his arm. Oh well. But this guy, I get this guy. What I don't understand is the rush, but that's his choice, his pain.

Over the weeks I learned that while his credit card says Peter everyone calls him Ray. As in a ray of sunshine or something like that. Not that I could tell he was a ray of sunshine, he seldom spoke at all except to ask if we were on schedule. He paid his bills, so who am I to complain.

By the last day, Ray could barely tolerate the needle, but we did manage to finish his design. I tried to put him off a few times, even a day or two, but he insisted we finished by noon today. At 11:30, I put in the last bit of shading. It was a good thing that the day was sunny and warm since he couldn't stand to put his shirt back on. He paid for the last of the work and left without saying a word. I decided to follow, it was lunchtime after all. Besides, his large Silverado was easy to shadow from a distance with my Harley.

At the edge of town, Ray pulled into the county cemetery and stopped behind a monument company truck. The workers were lifting a new headstone. They wave as Ray walks up. With great care, the workers and Ray place the stone on the foundation. From my vantage, I can see that the back of the headstone is only engraved with Ray's last name. Ray inspects the headstone and shakes the worker's hands as they pack up to leave.

Once they're gone Ray walks back around to the front of the stone. To respect his privacy, I circle around behind him. By that time, Ray is on his knees, one hand on the stone, the other covering his eyes. The craftsmanship of the stone's carving is wonderful. Etched into the stone is the image of a sleeping infant on a bed of rose petals under a blanket of fluffy clouds. The script beneath reads "In Memory of Jessica, July 14, 2012." It is the exact same image that I inked onto Ray's back.

I swear that what I saw next really happened, I didn't imagine it. As I stood there, a third image became visible, I don't know how to describe it. I guess I was seeing Ray's heart, not the pump thing, but his soul. And tattooed there was the exact same image of his back and the headstone. But as he wept beside her grave, his tattooed heart changed ever so slightly. It seemed like the clouds parted enough to let a beam of light shine on the infant's smile. It was there for only a moment, and then the image was gone. I left quietly, I didn't even start the Harley until I was near the cemetery's exit. Good thing it was all downhill.

Ray dropped by earlier today. I had emailed him about coming over so I could see if he needed any touch-ups since the swelling is down by now. I also wanted to get a picture for my book if he'd let me. While I was looking over the ink it happened again. The soul thing from the cemetery. Only this time the sunbeam was larger and covered Baby Jessica's face. Then it hit me. What the headstone guys carve into stone is forever. And I can't wipe away the ink on Ray's back. But God can heal a tattooed heart.

THE FOUNTAIN

When the weather is clear and the sun warm, people gather around Andrew's Fountain. There's something about its simple white marble columns and splashing water that attracts a crowd. Some choose to sit on the rim of the receiving pond and run their hands through the cool water. Others sit on the benches surrounding the fountain to watch it dance in the sunlight.

A middle-aged man in black pinstripe brags, "I tell you pork bellies are the way to go. Time it right and you can make a fortune."

"You're sure about that?" Sneers a similarly dressed older man. "Securities are much safer over the long haul. I've seen way too many lose their shirt on risky commodities."

"True, but when I hit it I'll be set for life, retire early and enjoy the sunshine," the younger trader replies.

"Never happen," mumbles the older trader while munching on another chip from his bag.

"Mom, can we go to the zoo now?" a young girl in a pink dress begs. The mother and two children rest on a bench near the traders. "Please?!"

"In a little while," the mother answers. "What do you think of the fountain? When I was your age, Aunt Martha would bring me here and we'd sit for hours watching the water."

"It's boring, elephants are better. Right, Joey?" The girl in pink asks her younger brother.

"I kind of like the water," he replies, earning him a nasty look from his sister.

"That's enough now," Mom scolds.

A few benches down sit an older couple. "Do you remember this spot?" asks the elderly man bent with age.

"Why Herman, of course, I remember. It may have been fifty-three years ago, but I remember it well." The grey-haired woman next to him replies. "It was dark and the lights were on in the fountain."

"We drove up before they put in the Interstate, it took four hours, but we made it," he continues.

"We ate at that Hot Dog stand for lunch and toured the museum," she adds.

"It was all I could afford," he confesses.

"Then we strolled along the riverfront watching the city folk hurry home," she recalls.

"We sat right here, boy was I nervous," he said.

"I couldn't tell," she said, resting her hand on his.

"Then I asked..." he said.

"And I said yes," she replies.

"Please, mom, can we go to the zoo now?" The girl in pink begs using the best puppy dog eyes she can muster.

"Soon, dear, soon," the mom sighs. "Let's finish lunch and watch the water a bit longer."

"Come on Chelsea, turn around and dangle your feet in the water," an older teenage boy encourages.

"Won't we get in trouble?" replies a girl of the same age.

"Naw, I've done it a bunch of times. Come on, it will be fine."

As the teens swirl their legs in the cool water, a large man in a dirty green jacket and unkempt hair walks up. "Excuse me, could you help a fellow out?" he mutters not daring to look them in the face.

The boy whirls around, "Go back to the shelter, let them take care of you."

The vagrant doesn't reply but walks around the fountain to the two businessmen. "Could you help a fellow out?" he asks.

"You'll only waste it on booze," the older trader spits.

"Why don't you get a job," the younger one sneers, throwing the rest of his lunch in the garbage.

The mom, seeing the vagrant, decides that visiting the zoo isn't such a bad idea after all. She quickly gathers the girl in pink and the younger brother and scoots them away from the man in the dirty green jacket.

The older couple, having watched and listened the whole time, wave the man closer. "Say, where did you get that jacket? Bit warm, don't you think?" the old man asks without giving him a chance to answer. "What's your name?"

"Bud, just call me Bud," the homeless man

mumbles.

"My eyes aren't as good as they used to be Bud, but there were patches on that jacket. Right?"

"Yeah, I wore it back from 'Nam."

"I thought so, I thought so," the old man coos. "Korea myself, let me shake your hand. This here is Martha and I'm Herman we're from downstate a ways. So, I heard you asking these fine citizens for help, mind if I ask what you're needing?"

"I'd like to go home, my mom is dying, I'm trying to raise bus fare," Bud confesses.

"I'm sorry to hear that, where does she live?" Martha asks.

"Plotterville, I doubt you know where that is. It's a small town a few miles south of..."

"Walnut Grove," Herman interjects, "We're a bit north of there, near Devan." Herman glances at Martha and sees her soft nod. "Tell you what, this is our last stop on memory lane, how about we give you a lift?"

"I couldn't," Bud replies, shaking his head. "It's too far."

"Sure, you could!" Herman encourages. "One old army vet to another."

"Marine, I was a Marine like my dad," Bud mutters.

"You ARE a Marine, no such things as was and I'm not taking no for an answer. Do you need to get anything?" Herman asks.

"Nope, this is it," Bud replies, exposing his empty hands.

The fountain splashes and plays in the sunlight while Herman, Martha, and Bud amble off.

Others soon take their place to soak in the sunshine while the water splashes against the white marble columns. Few ever notice the small brass plaque at the fountain's base – Andrew's Fountain. Dedicated 1909. For with thee is the fountain of life: in thy light shall we see light. Psalm 36:9

BENJAMIN ZOOK

"Benjamin Zook Carter! Put the tablet away and get down here right now!" a harried black mother called from the kitchen. "Breakfast is on the table and we have to go in five minutes!"

Ben knew how far to push it and mom had just activated the panic button by using his full name. A name he hated. He bounded downstairs and began shoveling his mom's pancakes into his mouth. Between his fourth and fifth forkful, he said, "Mom, can I ask you something?" Without pausing, "How come you called me Benjamin Zook and not something cool like Kayne or Keshan?"

"How old are you? Eight?" Mom asked.

"Come on, Mom, you know I'll be ten next week."

"Ten, well I guess it's time you ask your granddaddy about your name. How about we go see him next Saturday for your birthday?"

"Fun!" Ben replied after finishing the last of the pancake.

"Hi, Dad," Ben's mom yelled as she walked into the small apartment.

"Ho ho, looks who's here. Let me see you. Pretty as ever" as Ben's mom hugged granddaddy's bent frame. "And you, Benjamin, I wouldn't have known you. So tall now. Let's see you must be thirteen."

"I'm ten today, granddaddy," Ben corrected.

"My, my, that's right," Granddaddy replied with a twinkle in his eye.

"Dad?" Ben's mom began. "Benjamin doesn't like his name."

"Oh, really? So, you think it's time he heard the story?" Grandaddy asked. "Well, I knew the day would come. Let's sit around the table. Lemonade?"

A few moments later, with tall glasses of lemonade in front of them, Granddaddy asked: "So why don't you like your name?"

"It's not like the other black kids. Deaza says that it's a slave name and that I should have an African sounding name."

"Uh, huh," granddaddy nodded. "I understand that. Some of our people have the name of their ancestor's master. Others took white-sounding names to fit in better. But not you, no sir. What do you think my name is?"

"I don't know," Ben acknowledged, "your just granddaddy."

"Well, my name is Benjamin Zook Harrison. Sound familiar?"

"So, I'm named after you?" Ben asks.

"Yes and no. You see, I'm named after my great-great-great-grandfather, who was a slave."

"And he was named by his master? See Deaza's right." Ben interjected.

"Let me tell you about it then you can tell me if you still want to be called Benjamin Zook," Grandaddy answered.

This was, of course, a long time ago, somewhere around 1853. Several years before the Civil War and President Lincoln's Emancipation Proclamation. Let's keep this simple and say your great-granddaddy instead of trying to get the right number of greats in there. Anyway, your great-granddaddy was a field slave on a plantation in Mississippi. One day he ran away and went north. Now I don't know all the details. I know he came north, but he couldn't find a way to cross where the Illinois flows into the Mississippi River. So, he followed the Illinois awhile and crossed the river at the narrows south of Peoria.

No one is quite sure where but one night he holed up in a dairy barn and was discovered early the next morning. Now rumor had it that if a runaway slave could find the Quakers, they would help them get to Canada and freedom. But your great-granddaddy had never met a Quaker, all he knew is that they talked strangely and dressed plain. The farmer who found him seemed to fit the bill with his plain clothes and impossible to understand language. But he wasn't Quaker, but German Mennonite.

The farmer and his wife offered your great-grandad food and a place to shelter to regain his strength. But unlike the Quakers, the Mennonites were divided on what to do with runaway slaves. They had experienced their own conflicts in the old country having been hunted and persecuted for a time. The last thing they wanted was to create trouble with the law. Yet, their religion and especially the Parable of the Good Samaritan told them to help this man.

A few days later, the farmer and your granddad

attended a meeting of the elders at their meetinghouse. That's what they called their church building. The way I heard it passed down, there was quite an argument. One side wanted to obey the state and turn your great-granddaddy over to the sheriff. Others wanted to take him to a Quaker settlement a few days ride north.

Your great-granddaddy, tired of the voices he couldn't understand, went out to rest against the side of the building. One of the younger Mennonites, a son of one of the elders, soon joined him in the sunshine. This younger one spoke clearer English and explained to your grandpa what was going on.

They sat and talked for a while comparing their experiences until a young boy ran around the corner. It seemed that a slave-hunter had gotten wind of the meeting and was on his way to collect his prize. Your granddaddy was ready to run, but the young Mennonite had a better idea and hid your granddaddy in the muck of an outhouse. This was before plumbing. Outhouses were simple sheds built over a deep hole where folks went to relieve themselves. It was smelly, dirty, and fly-infested.

Your grandpa found out later that the slave-hunters invasion galvanized the Mennonite elders. When asked where your grandpa was hiding at, they all stood silent. The slave-hunter threatened and cajoled them trying to find an opening in their wall of silence. He waved shackles in their faces and threatened to burn the place down. The younger Mennonite stepped forward and asked: "How much to buy the runaway?" This caused a stir. To own a slave was forbidden in their fellowship, what was this young man doing?

The slave-hunter thought for a moment. "Tell you what, I need a horse, a good draft horse to haul a wagon of captured slaves back to Mississippi. I'll trade you a horse for the slave." This caused even more discussion among the elders. To help the slave-hunter seemed to be an even bigger sin. Your granddaddy found out later that the young man was recently married and only had the one horse. "Yes," the young man replied, and a deal was struck.

That young Mennonite retrieved your grandpa from the outhouse. A few days later he hired a lawyer to write up the writ of manumission which made your granddaddy a freedman. When the lawyer was writing the document, he asked for your great-granddaddy's name. Your great-granddaddy didn't want to carry his slave name any longer, so he named himself after the young man that bought his freedom, Benjamin Zook.

"You see Benjamin? Your name is special. I hope someday when you have a son, you'll also honor the man that bought our freedom." Granddaddy concluded.

"Benjamin Zook," the youngster whispered, rolling his name on his tongue as if to see how it tasted. "Wait until Deaza here's this!" He announced.

THE BIKER AND THE BEES

It was one of those days. The gang fight at Block 98, home of the Midnight Riders Motorcycle Club, was the talk of every alley, tenement, and dark shadow. The fight looked to be a straight-up turf war between the Riders and the Aces. Somehow a third gang became involved, one new to the streets. Rumor has it they're an all-girl gang called the Bees. Everything else is rumor and guesses made worse by the fog of gossip.

Every customer visiting my tattoo parlor has their ideas about what went down. None of them the same. Now, I try to keep my business neutral between the various biker gangs, some of them are my best customers. It's not easy, but this means I do have hooks into each of them. So, while the streets mull over the rumor, I take my Harley to find the truth.

My first stop is Block 98, a dive bar on the west side where it all went down. It's a typically seedy place in a run-down neighborhood. It is, however, the only cement block building in sight. Dreary. No windows. It's one door races the walls to see who will be the first to shed their ancient layers of paint. No one knows what the 98 means, no one really cares.

To my surprise, there were cops everywhere. Street fights between rival gangs usually garner little attention. I knew things were bad when I saw the yellow "Police Line Do Not Cross" tape. I spy one of my customers, a city cop I know as Chad, who is guarding a spot on the line. I wheel up and cut the Harley's rumble.

"What's up, Chad?" I ask.

"I can't tell you much Red, we're under orders to keep it quiet until the next of kin are notified," Chad replies.

"So, someone kicked off? Still, it's a lot of cops and brass for a gang brawl, even if one did die. Can you tell me how many died and which gang?"

"Sorry, no. Orders."

"Anyone else get hurt?"

"A few of the Midnight Riders were taken to St. Luke's and a couple of Aces to Methodist. The Captain ordered it that way in case there was any fight left in them."

I wanted to ask more, but my radar told me that I was making the brass nervous. The Harley rumbled back to life and I steered it towards downtown where both hospitals sit within spitting distance of each other.

Somewhere between Perry and Adams, I decided to steer towards Methodist first. No particular reason other than the twisties heading onto their campus. The Aces are a rough and tumble gang with more bark than bite. Something must have set them off to tackle the Midnight Riders on their home turf.

I hate ERs. If you're not sick yet, you're guaranteed to catch the latest bug before you leave. Bad for business, no one wants a skin artist with a runny nose to ink them. Luckily one of the Aces is right inside the door and I was able to pull him outside. Spider is mid-level in their organization. He's their procurer of slightly used parts at a discount. Ok, he's a thief. But he's always paid for my services, so we're square.

"How bad was it Spider?"

"Pretty normal slugfest, a few broken noses, cuts and such." He chuckles before continuing, "Slash broke his hand. He swung at one of the Riders and missed. His fist tried to KO a post. The post won."

"Ouch. Cops said someone died, one of yours?" I ask.

"Naw, we were having a good time of it when a bunch of chicks show up and try to break up the fun. One of them went down. You say she died? That's bad business."

"I'm not sure who died, but the cops are all over it. So, who started it?" I ask.

"You know how these things go Red. They do something on our turf, we do something on theirs. No starting, just continuing."

"Yep, I hear you. Any idea where the girl gang came from? Who they are?"

"I didn't get a good look. Once the gun went off, we all bugged out. Don't even bother asking about the gun, I only heard it. A lot of us were packing, but it's like a rule, fists, knives, and clubs. Hurt, but don't kill."

"Thanks, man," I say, closing our little session with

a fist bump. Spider confirmed much that I had already suspected, but the big questions remained. Who is this new all-girl gang, why did they show up, and exactly what happened?

Ten minutes later, I'm outside St. Luke's ER trying to build up another batch of courage. I hope to catch a Midnight Rider like I did Spider. No such luck. Walking through the waiting room, I spy Ranger in a dark corner by the vending machines. Ranger is Midnight Rider's top dog, and he has the scars to prove it. I know because I've inked him more than once. The Ranger I see is not the Ranger I know. He's always big and alert. You know he's in the room, everyone does. But at this moment he looks small and defeated, slumped in a dark corner on a hard-plastic chair.

"It's all my fault," I hear him mutter as I slide into the seat next to him.

"Hey, Ranger, you ok?" I ask.

"No, yes. I'm not hurt if that's what you mean," Ranger says looking up. "Hey, Red."

"What's your fault? What happened?"

Now biker gang leaders and tears don't go together, but that's the sight I see. "Come on, man, tell me about it. It's ok."

"It's all my fault. She's gone, one of the few who ever cared is gone." Ranger sobbed.

Now my counseling skills are zero. I'm a poop or get off the pot kind of person with no patience and darn little compassion. Those are a required skill set in my line of work. But I had another one of those vision things like Ray's tattooed heart. It was just a glimpse, but I saw a grandma type sitting on Ranger's other side cradling his head.

"Was it your grandma? I don't get it?" I stammer.

"I never knew my grandparents or my parents. Not my real ones, anyway." He paused and then chuckled. "Yeah, I guess she is, was, a bit like I imagined a grandma to be."

"Go on," I encourage.

"Where to start? Let me think," Ranger mutters.

"I was riding solo one Saturday morning a few months back, trying to clear my head by taking country roads. I'd heard there were some twisties not far off the river road."

"Banta?"

"Yeah, that's it. If you've ridden it then you know it dumps you out on top of the bluff with nothing but straight flat prairie roads in front of you. I just kept going and found a good stretch for a flat out run to see what the bike could give me. It topped out at over 110, but the bike didn't like it. She started running rough, and I managed to limp her into a place called Fairlawn."

"Never heard of it."

"No reason you should have. It may have been something before the railroad pulled out, but now there's only a handful of small houses and an old church. There were a few cars at the church, so I figured it was the best place to find a phone."

"No cell phone?"

"No. I hate those things, just one interruption after another. Anyway, sure enough, the church is unlocked. When I step in, I hear laughter. Like angels laughing that

I'd dare to set foot in God's house. I've always bragged that when I show up at the pearly gates, God will laugh as He throws me to hell."

Ranger pauses a beat.

"I told myself to pull it together and find the people. The laughter led me to the basement. Around a table sat seven older ladies sewing a quilt. I've never seen anything quite like it. The pattern was amazing. All blues and white with hundreds of triangles and squares arranged to look like a lion. They didn't see me, so I fake coughed to get their attention. I must have been a menacing sight. Black leathers, biker gloves, and my bald head covered by a flaming skull dew rag. 'I'm looking for a phone.' I growled. One of them came over and introduced herself as Anne."

"There's a phone in the kitchen, cell service doesn't work out here," Anne offered. "Would you like some breakfast strudel and some coffee?"

"Sure, I guess so," I muttered. "That's some beautiful work," I said, pointing at the quilt.

"Red, you know I like designing. I made our logo and drew several of the tatts you've done. That quilt was something."

"We call ourselves the Bees, as in quilting bee. This quilt is going to an orphanage in Ukraine that our church partners with," Anne explains.

"Long story short I make the phone call and Shorty heads out to pick me up. In the meantime, the Bees show me more of their work. All of it amazing. The next Saturday, I end up back in the church basement. Imagine me with a group of grey-haired grandmothers eating breakfast strudel and quilting. I've been back every

Saturday since. Onc Saturday I even brought some of other Midnight Riders and gave the Bees a ride to Al's Drive-In for lunch. That was a sight to see."

"So, what happened today?" I asked, trying to get us back on track.

"Anne called a few days ago and asked to meet up with the gang at Block 98. The Bees had finished a quilt with our logo and they wanted to present it to us. Before the Bees showed up, the Aces barged in ready for a brawl. It seems that one of my guys trespassed on their territory. So, we go at it. About five minutes later, the Bees walk in, but instead of running away, they try to break up the fight. Lefty Louie, my second in command, pulls his Colt to shoot the ceiling and call a truce. The Ace's second sees the move and must think that Lefty is escalating. They struggle for the Colt, it goes off. There's a pause, a freeze-frame. Anne slumps, a red stain painting her blouse. Everyone scatters. Everyone except for Anne, me, and a few of the boys too hurt to run."

"I rushed to Anne, cradled her head, and tried to stop the bleeding. She smiled and breathed her last. She smiled Red! I've seen folks die before, but not one of them ever smiled. Not ever."

I've thought a lot about that day. About Anne and the Bees. How they accepted someone in their circle so completely different from them. What haunted me most was Ranger's report about Anne's smile. I never knew her, although I have gotten to know a few of the Bees. The question about what happened at Block 98 is solved, but now I have a new mystery. Why did Anne smile?

Seasons of Forgiveness: Autumn

THE OAK LEAF

"One more shelf Emily and we'll be done" Dad encourages. While not grueling work, cleaning out Mom's closet is emotionally draining. It took Dad a few years to be ready for it, I know that I'm not. We are both a little wary of this last shelf, its where she stored her keepsakes. The home of her most treasured memories.

We remove each box and explore its contents with care. Several are filled with greeting cards, both store-bought and handmade. Some of them make us laugh, a few make us cry. Another box contains trinkets from various destinations around the country. A thimble from the Grand Canyon. A silver spoon from Wall Drug Store. A Minnie Mouse hat – somewhere there's a picture of Mom and me sporting our hats. The last shoebox I pull from the shelf is so light I thought it may be empty. "Watcha got Emily?" Dad asks.

"I'm not sure," I say and hand Dad the old shoebox. With slow deliberateness, he removes the lid and peers

63

inside. "I forgot about these," he whispers. Stepping down from the kitchen chair, I look in the box for myself. It seems to be a collection of dried leaves. Reaching to pick one of them up, I ask, "why'd she keep these Dad?"

"Careful Emily, they'll be very fragile by now," Dad advises as he put the lid back on. "Let's go get some tea and I'll explain."

After settling around the kitchen table, Dad again opens the box. "These leaves are from Deer Run Park. You remember our fall hikes?"

"You mean with all of Mom's family? Sure."

Dad leans back and begins to reminisce, "They'd pick a weekend in October, hoping that the leaves had turned. We would drive the couple hours to the park to picnic and hike no matter the weather. Some years were beautiful. The bright sun causing the trees to glow with color. It always reminded me of a patchwork quilt. Other years it was cold and gloomy. But there was a special beauty in that as well." Sitting forward, Dad turns to me. "Each hike your Mom would gather a leaf, one that she found to be the prettiest or special in some way."

"I remember that. You used to get so perturbed because she would stop on the trail to look for leaves while everyone else hiked on.

"Yeah, well, she was not happy with any old leaf, it had to be just right." Dad examined the box for a few moments. "She could pick up each one of these and tell you which hike it was from. Not always what year but something related.

"Like the year the park was so flooded we had to wade through the last part to finish the trail?"

"Yeah, something like that. She could tell you which leaf she collected that year, but I can't."

"So what are we going to do with them? We can't throw them out or burn them like other leaves." Both of us stare at the box as if it held the answer.

Stirring in his chair, Dad says, "Let's take them back. How about you and I take these back to Deer Run."

"Are your knees up to it? If I remember right, some of those trails were pretty rugged."

"I'll be alright, we can stay on the easier trails. I've heard there's a way down to the dells that avoid the stairs. Does the third Saturday in October work for you? We always went around that time."

"The third Saturday it is," I confirm.

Following an uneventful drive, we finally reach the park entrance. Sunshine lights the trees along the entrance creating the feel of stained glass. After a brief picnic of sub sandwiches and chips, we begin our walk. Dad is dressed for the hike as I always remembered, blue jeans, a denim jacket, a broad brim hat, and a walking stick. The one difference is the shoebox held in his other arm.

"So how are we going to do this?" I asked as we entered the trail.

"How about we place a leaf in places Mom would have liked it?"

"Okay, sounds good to me." As we hike along, we can hear the giggling of children ahead. Every now and again, the wind would rustle the trees causing a colorful cascade of leaves to drift down.

"That looks like a good place," gently taking a leaf from the box, Dad points to a boulder by the stream. "Put

65

this one by the boulder Emily." Returning from my task, I see him smile and nod, pleased with the spot. As we walk the trail memories bubble to the surface. Dad recalls my first hike. I remember the time my uncles got lost. We both laugh at the place aunt Marie fell in the creek. Every now and then Dad stops, hands me a leaf and points out a rock, a peculiar tree, or a bright spot where the sun is breaking through the trees. Dad smiles and nods each time a leaf is placed.

"Well Emily, we're down to the last leaf," he says holding up a very brittle oak leaf. "This was probably her first leaf, maybe from when she was a kid. We need to find someplace special."

We came across several promising spots, an old stump, a small patch of wildflowers, a bed of pine needles, and a peculiarly twisted maple. But none of them are exactly perfect. At one point, Dad mentions putting it in the stream that runs beside the trail, but that doesn't quite fit either. Rounding a bend in the trail we enter the dells, we'll soon have to turn back. This part of the trail runs between sandstone cliffs. Damp, dark, and musty this section is different than the rest of the trail. At the end of the dells are ladders which continue the trail but will it be the end of the line for us. Along the dells were various cul-de-sacs with fantastic names like "Devil's Punchbowl" and "Giant's Bathtub." In one nameless cul-de-sac, there is a shelf-like space worn into the sandstone. It was the place where Mom's family always stopped to capture a family photo. We called it the "caves" even though the only cave-like feature was a hole the kids could go through.

The "sitting in the caves" photos in Mom's albums

tumble through my mind. They're all similar. Yet together they mark the passing of time. Children growing up. New faces as soon to be spouses make their first hike and the smaller faces of grandchildren. Looking at the caves, I can almost see them jostling around for another picture. This is the perfect spot for the last leaf.

"Emily, crawl up there. Find a crack or a spot where the wind won't blow it away." Dad says as he hands me the leaf. Near the back of the shelf, I find a small opening between the layers of rock. Using a twig, I gently prod the leaf into the crack. Clambering down from the shelf, I see Dad smile, nod, and knock the remaining bits of leaf from the box.

"Very good Emily, I think Mom would approve. How about we head to the General Store from some ice cream?"

Taking the shoebox, I link my arm in his and together we begin to walk back the way we came. About halfway back, I stop, reach down and pick up a perfect deep red oak leaf. Twirling it by the stem I examine its form, its veins, the richness of its color. When I hold it up to the sun it glows like stained glass. Opening up the shoebox I place it inside.

"Watcha doing Emily?" Dad asks.

"I think that it may be time to start keeping some memories of my own, is it okay if I keep the shoebox?" Dad smiles, nods, and together, we walk back.

THE APPLESEED GOSPEL

One autumn afternoon, Matt decided to pedal his bike around the section to see how harvest was going. Well, that's what he told his ma. His real objective was to check on Mr. Bright's apples and "borrow" a few if they're ready.

Along the way, Matt checked on the neighbor's fields. Of interest was Mr. Patterson's pumpkin patch. The factory workers would soon flock to the field. They'd row the pumpkins with one kind of machine and lift them into the back of trucks with another strange-looking machine. Mr. King already had his corn in Matt noted as he turned the northeast corner. But across the road, old Johnny Darst's corn was still standing. Another mile, a few more fields, and Matt came upon Mr. Bright's place.

Laying his bike in the ditch, Matt climbed the wire fence and dropped into Mr. Bright's pasture. A few of the grazing sheep looked up and wondered about the intruder but soon went back to their sweet grass. The apple tree stood in the middle of the pasture. Unlike modern dwarf varieties, this tree was a good 30 feet tall and loaded with deep red apples. Matt picked a few of the low hanging fruit and sat with his back to the trunk and his face to the road. It was a relaxing, satisfying, content moment away from schoolwork, chores, and siblings.

"Hello there," Matt heard with a start, his quiet moment turning towards shock and fear. A big hand settled on his shoulder. "Didn't mean to scare you so, I thought you heard me coming." Matt had met Mr. Bright several times and he always looked the same. Thin as a blade of grass and taller than most. He always seemed to have on the same bib overalls and the same worn-out Dekalb seedcorn hat. It was his eyes that Matt noticed most because they always seemed to take in everything that was around. "Looks like you've been helping yourself to some of my apples. How are they this year?"

"Uh," Matt said, looking into those eyes, "they're fantastic."

"Good, I thought they might be ready." Mr. Bright pulls a plastic bag from his pocket and hands it to Matt. "Feel free to take some home."

"You're, you're not mad at me?" Matt asked

"I'm a little disappointed you didn't feel the need to ask me first, but I forgive you," Mr. Bright said plucking an apple. "These are mighty tempting after all."

"You can say that again," Matt said.

Sitting on the ground next to Matt, Mr. Bright asked, "Anybody ever tell you the apple seed gospel?"

"I don't think so, I mean, I've heard about Matthew, Mark, Luke, and John."

"Well, this is kinda related. It's another way to say the same thing." Mr. Bright rubbed the apple against his

70

pants, giving a glow to the apple's dark red skin. "Pretty thing ain't it. These red ones always remind me of Jesus. The color is so dark it reminds me of my sins and the blood of Jesus that washed them away." Taking a bite from the apple, "my that's good." Turning the apple so that Matt could see the inside. "But while the outside is red, the inside is white, untainted and pure." Jesus didn't go to the cross because of His own sin but because of ours. We're more like that rotting apple over there." Mr. Bright kicked at one of the fallen apples that had begun to turn brown. "But that's what Jesus does, takes an old fallen, bruised, rotting apple and makes them like new again."

"But what about the apple seeds? You said this was the apple seed gospel."

"So I did," Mr. Bright replied. "Go pick me out another apple." While Matt wandered the tree looking for the best one, Mr. Bright retrieved a pocket knife from his overalls. Matt soon returned with a beautiful one and handed it to Mr. Bright. "Nope, you hold onto it. Take this knife and cut it in half around the middle."

"Hey look, there's a star," Matt exclaimed.

"Yep, every apple has that five-pointed star. In one sense, it reminds me of the star that guided the wise men to Bethlehem. But it also tells me that God has given every person five things, five seeds for them to plant and care for. The first seed is life, only God can give life. We may help it along a bit at times, but it all starts with God. The second seed is love, God loved us first; long before we even understood it. The third seed is faith, God grants to each person a seed of faith to follow His word. The fourth seed is time, or you could say eternity. While time starts and

71

stops what God has given us extends beyond time. The last seed is purpose as in God's unique plan for each of us. Follow so far?"

"Yeah, I think so," Matt replied, examining the five-pointed star.

"So, what do you think God wants you to do with those seeds?" Mr. Bright asked.

"I don't know, plant them?"

"Right, God wants us to plant the seeds He gives us. Too often we simply throw them away. Kind of like today. In a way, you threw away a seed of love by choosing to take apples without asking me. But let me ask you this, how many seeds are in an apple?"

"Five," Matt replied.

"Okay, how many apples are in a seed?"

"Uh," Matt said his mind beginning to reel with the possibilities. "I guess only God could figure that one out," he finally answered.

"Right! Our job is to plant seeds and watch them grow. There's a Bible verse that comes to mind. "I planted, Apollos watered, but God was causing the growth. So then neither the one who plants nor the one who waters is anything, but God who causes the growth." You see, you threw a seed away today, but I planted one by forgiving you."

"Oh, I'm sorry, Mr. Bright, I should have asked you first.

"Like I said, you are forgiven by both me and God. How about we fill that bag so you can take some of these fantastic apples back to your family?"

THE HUNTER

The mark was easy. A country hick that wandered into the wrong alley of City Center, my alley. So, I welcomed him to our crusty city by relieving him of his bulging wallet and cheap watch. I didn't even have to pull out Bertha, my six-inch bowie knife. The threat alone had him shaking like a California earthquake.

I can hear the sirens already; the rube must have called 911 from Sam's Corner Deli. No worries, there are plenty of alleys, backstreets, and dark corners in my hunting grounds.

Tucked in a shadow of another alley I watch as my most recent benefactor recreates his story for two patrol officers. I almost laughed out loud when he stands in my footprints and tries to look like me. I'm more menacing than I thought. Good.

"There is no fear of God in your eyes," a voice said with the grating tone of a broken clarinet reed. Turning from the comedy across the street, I see one of the dozen or so homeless hags that scramble for what others throw away. They are useful to me as they putter along the streets of City Center. Residents take no notice of them but out of towners always react in predictable ways. Some with visible revulsion, others with compassion. Those compassionate ones are my best prey.

"What did you say, old woman?" I growl. I do have to keep the natives in line from time to time. "Were you talking to me or just babbling some old nonsense?"

She turned from her dumpster diving and looked me in the eye. With that same grating voice, she said, "there is no fear of God in your eyes."

"There is no god," I growled as I pulled Bertha from the sheath. I dodged around a pile of pallets and slipped into a sliver of sunshine. She needed to see who I was and the danger she was in. "There is no god to fear or worship only hunters, prey, and those that grovel on the ground."

"There is no fear of God in your eyes," she repeated with more firmness than before. Our eyes locked. Her will is stronger than I imagined. I moved a few steps closer and made sure she could see Bertha's cold edge. As I did so, her eyes widened and then closed in laughter.

"Officers! There he is!" I heard as if a loudspeaker had aimed all its power down the alley. "He's got a knife!" I heard the footsteps and felt the officer's shadow darken the alley. I froze, there was no escape. Nowhere to run. Nowhere to hide. "Drop the knife!" one officer yelled. "On the ground, get on the ground!" another bellowed. I did as they ordered, there was no other option. The hunter became prey.

The rube identified me. The police collected his

wallet and watch from my pocket. Bertha became bagged and tagged evidence. For six years, I hunted City Center without being caught or suspected. My Public Aid Lawyer managed to get a plea deal which landed me five years, three if I behave myself. But that's not the end of the story.

I've done time before. Not much though, this was the longest stretch so far. Thirty days as a Juvenile, 90 days in the county lockup at the small town where I grew up. This stretch was harder, even though it was only a medium-security state prison. I survived by falling back into my world of hunters, prey, and grovelers.

About a year in everything changed. I had worked my way in with those I call hunters. We ran the place. The guards didn't care so long as there was peace and we were all good little prisoners doing what they said. They were good with it if peace took an occasional beat down, the periodic theft, the random embarrassment, or worse.

We all had jobs, mine was in the laundry. Every day all I did was load and unload the giant machines for eight hours a day. Exactly how that was to prepare me for the outside world, I still don't understand. But I did my job aiming to get out as soon as possible.

Like every other day for the past few months, I was loading and unloading when one of the pushers rolled his large hamper my way. I had pegged him as a groveler early on. Young, stupid, and out of his depth. Drug charge or so they say.

"Your Kirk, right?" he asked in a soft voice I had trouble hearing over the machines.

"Yea," I muttered, "So?"

"Well, I have a word from the Lord for you," He

said with a trace of tremor in his voice.

I thought about making an example of him but boredom and curiosity combined against me. "Ok, so spit it out. Tell me what the big guy has to say," I mocked.

"Umm, God says 'hi'" he said, looking everywhere but me.

"That's it? No big pronouncement of how evil I am? Or how much He supposedly loves me? Just 'Hi'?"

"Umm, yea. That's it," The shakiest jailbird laundry pusher in the world replied.

Ok, I'll play along. "Well tell the big guy 'hi' in return," I said with a small chuckle and a shake of my head.

He left without saying a word. In fact, he didn't say anything to me for the rest of the day as he brought loads for my hungry washing machines. Come to think of it this was the first time I'd ever heard him speak at all.

The next day the scene repeated itself with the word being "I know you." My response back was, "know what about me?" I expected the jailbird to launch into a monologue, but he left as silent as before. The third day the word was, "I know everything from the number of hairs on your head to the many scars left by your father."

I turned with sudden anger on the jailbird. "You've been spying on me! Watching me in the shower or something. God isn't telling you anything, you've seen my scars," I yell cocking a fist to cause him some permanent pain.

"No, no," he whimpered. "I'm in D block, you're in C, the only places I've ever seen you are here, the yard, and eating. God told me those words."

"I don't believe you, then someone else told you."

"You've seen me around, I don't talk to anyone. Ever."

That much was true. The guy was a mouse. Keeping his head down and mouth shut, hoping to stay off everyone's radar. Classic groveler.

"Even if I did see your scars, which I haven't, I wouldn't know that your dad caused them," the jailbird offered.

My arm relaxed as that bit of light cut through the darkness of my soul. No one knows except for me. "God told you about my scars? About my dad?"

"No, He only gave me the words to say. I've been praying for you. Praying for a lot of the guys in here. I did some stupid things, but landing here changed my life. Brought me back to Jesus and took away all the things I thought were important but weren't. Even so, it took me a week to work up the courage to give you the first message." Something changed in him while he said this. He went from the shaking mouse that couldn't look me in the eye to a confident man looking into my soul.

"Hey, you! Get back to work!" a guard barks.

"Let's talk tonight, C block commons," I whisper. He nods and pushes his cart out of the laundry.

That was the beginning of a new life. Today I'm back in City Center for the first time since my arrest. New job, new look, even a new outlook. I would have been back sooner, but a condition of my parole was that I stay away from my old hunting grounds.

I savor every morsel of a Pastrami on Rye at Sam's Deli before my next call. My job isn't glamorous, but it does keep me busy. I'm one of those copier repair guys. So,

I settle my bill with Sam and head out with my briefcase-style repair kit.

Crossing the same alley I was arrested in, I just had to look. To remember that day and the old woman with her cryptic words. As I walk deeper in I sense movement in the shadows.

"Well, well, well. Said the spider to the fly," I turned and saw a figure emerge from the shadow. "I don't know why you entered my web, but it's going to cost you. Hand over your wallet." The figure said with the familiar threatening stance.

I laughed, "Not much there I'm afraid, but you're welcome to it" and threw the wallet at his feet.

He picked it up and rifled through it. "five bucks? That's it? No credit cards? What's in the case?" He asks, hoping for a larger score.

"Only tools, screwdrivers and such, nothing worth fencing." I offered. "Say, I'm kind of new at this, so don't freak out or anything, but God wants to tell you something."

"Great, a religious nut," he mutters. "Go on, what does the big guy want?"

"God says 'hi'"

We stand there for a few moments. I think he expected more and I was waiting to see what he'd do next. It was one of those frozen in time moments that are a blink of an eye but feel like minutes.

"Everything alright? Is this man bothering you?" A Police officer asked from the entrance of the alley.

"Umm, no officer. Everything is fine. I dropped my wallet, and this fine gentleman is returning it to me," I replied. The mugger, following my lead, hands it back to me.

"Thanks, man," the mugger whispered. "Tell God, "hi" for me."

"You can do that yourself," I whispered back. "Thanks," I said at a more normal volume before the wannabe hunter slips out of the alley.

"Thanks, officer," I said, walking to the entrance.

"You sure you are ok? I know that guy and the trouble he causes," The officer said.

"No problem, officer."

"Say, don't I know you? You look familiar." The officer asked.

"Well, you did arrest me once. Actually, it was in this very alley about five years ago," I said, pointing back at the shadows.

The officer thought for a moment, "Yeah, that's it. You pulled a large knife on a homeless woman and had mugged a tourist."

"Sorry to say that was me. Say you don't know if that old homeless woman is still around?" I asked.

"No, she's long gone. You know how it is," The officer said. "Why do you ask?"

"Nothing big, I just wanted to tell her that I see things differently. That's all."

THE BRIDGE

In a land far from here, in a time long forgotten, there were two villages separated by a deep chasm. On the east side of the wide rocky gorge was Becket's Corner, to the west lay Paradise.

When the elder's grandfathers were young, a wobbly suspension bridge provided passage between the two villages. Over time, the villages grew apart. Each community blaming something the other had done.

Then, one night, the bridge was gone. Both sides pointed fingers at the other for its destruction, but neither could prove anything. While a few mourned the loss of the bridge most didn't seem to care. They were content, even happy, to be on their own.

One day in a far-off city, many years after the bridge fell, Jason from Becket's corner met Ferdinand from Paradise. At first, the old animosity and hatred ruled. They tried to avoid each other, but their orbits brought them together again and again.

Soon they found snippets of commonality. Jason introduced Ferdinand to fried sweet dough. Ferdinand shared his favorite spiced wine. Delights they both enjoyed. They told their stories. They laughed when the other recounted something upside down from their understanding. They got angry when a basic tenet was misunderstood. Yet through these shared moments over fried sweet dough and spiced wine, they built a bridge of sorts.

Eventually, the day came for Jason and Ferdinand to return to their villages. They each carried home the things they had shared. While the fried sweet dough and spiced wine were welcomed additions. Their new views of the village across the chasm were unwelcome.

At the dawning of each day, Jason and Ferdinand approached the chasm to talk with each other through the wig-wag waves of signal flags. Their times always ended with "WIBN" for wouldn't it be nice as they recalled sharing food, drink, and stories.

A few years later, news came to Paradise that war was marching across the land. Another people had invaded from across the sea and were burning villages as they marched toward the far-off city. Becket's Corner felt safe since the city would have to fall before the enemy could reach them. Many on the safe side laughed and danced at their good fortune. Jason mourned Paradise's unavoidable fate.

The citizens of Paradise considered many options. They thought about trying to race the enemy to the city, but that seemed impossible. Someone proposed hiding in the caves until another reminded them there wouldn't be any food after the invaders burned the village. Ferdinand suggested something unheard of, build a bridge to Becket's corner. Most everyone scoffed at the idea. The distance was too great. Becket's corner would turn them back or worse.

The next morning Ferdinand wig-waged the news to Jason. "hold," Jason replied, "I will see, back at noon." With that, Jason ran off. He talked to the elders and leaders of the village. It wasn't their problem, they replied. He talked to the oldest in the village to see if he could discover how they built the first bridge. A secret no one remembered. But Jason did find a few willing to help, a few men and women ready to do whatever they could.

At noon Jason signaled back. "Have a plan, get longest ropes possible. Back one hour."

"WIBN," Ferdinand replied and hurried off.

Ferdinand likewise found a few women and men willing to do something. After gathering several hundred feet of rope, Ferdinand and friends gathered at the chasm and signaled Jason.

In the meantime, Jason had also collected all the rope he could find. He put some to work setting the posts while others assembled the ropes into a bundle. Jason then tied two of the ropes to a post and a large stone to the other end. With some help, he threw the stone into the gorge. "Do the same," he signaled Ferdinand.

Once Ferdinand launched his stone, Jason signaled, "meet me." Taking a rope in hand, he repelled down the steep walls of the chasm. Ferdinand followed suit.

In the darkness of the steep-sided valley, the two friends hugged. Jason explained his plan and its requirements. They tied one of the ropes from each side together and scaled back up the chasm. Once both were again at the top, at Jason's signal, Ferdinand's friends began pulling on the joined rope. On the other end, Jason and friends knotted the bundle of ropes to the one heading towards Paradise.

It took many hours to complete, but soon a rudimentary three-line bridge spanned the chasm. A thick rope for the "floor" and two thinner ropes above on each side for something to hold onto. While all this was going on, villagers from both sides gathered at the chasm. Some cheering, some jeering, but most watched as the impossible became possible.

Jason and three leaders from Becket's Corner were the first to cross. While talks began between the leaders of the villages, work on more spans got underway. Soon there were three wobbly rope bridges across the chasm. Which both sides worked to lay wooden planking across. When the loose lumber ran out, folks began tearing wood from sheds, lean-tos, and even homes to provide the extra flooring needed.

By the time the last plank was set in place, the leaders from Becket's corner had agreed to house and feed the refugees. This was not as easy as it sounds. They fought over old animosities, but when a watchman reported a dust cloud in the distance, both sides knew it was now or never.

Fears were conquered that day. Many defeated their fear of the wobbly bridge. Others won over their fear of what they may find on the other side, but all made it over. The last of Paradise's leaders crossing as the invading hoard burnt the first of the outlying homes.

Everyone from both villages watched as the enemy

looted, plundered, and destroyed Paradise. Many wept, but none looked away. Ferdinand, Jason, and friends stood by with axes; ready to destroy the bridges they had just built. But the enemy had no interest in dividing their forces and soon left on their march towards the far-off city. They left nothing in Paradise but smoke, fire, and ash.

The citizens of Becket's corner and the refugees of Paradise buried a few of the old wounds that night. As time passed, more and more of those wounds healed as the villagers learned to accept one another, care for one another, and even love one another. And over time they improved, widened, and strengthened the bridge.

The next year, a new village called Paradise Corner was born. Some still preferred one side over the other. Some still chose to live a certain way. Some still saw things differently than the others, but they were now one people with a strong bridge.

Seasons of Forgiveness: Winter

THE NURSES HAT

The ambulance driver killed the siren as they rounded the comer of the St. Luke's Hospital and headed for the emergency room entrance. While lights still flashed the driver backed the ambulance into the designated area. There was already an ER crew standing by ready to receive the person in the ambulance. As soon as the wheels stopped, the back door of the ambulance flew open. The ER team rushed forward, retrieved a middle-aged man who had lost control of his pickup, and wheeled him into the emergency room.

On the way in, the EMT handed off some paperwork to one of the nurses. The nurse took a quick look at the driver's license and read the name – William Anderson – she froze. The ER doctor noticed and said, 'Amanda what are you doing, let's go, it's going to be close if we're going to save this guys life." Amanda didn't move. The ER doc continued down the hall and yelled, "AMANDA."

--

"Billy Anderson, I hate you," Amanda screamed at Billy's back as he ran away. Amanda had been walking to class when Billy ran up behind her and pushed her into a snowbank. Amanda and her books landed in the snow along with a report for Christian Doctrine she had worked most of the night to finish.

It was the latest in a long line of abuses that Billy had inflicted on Amanda. They were both seniors in the class of 1965, and Billy had been trouble for Amanda for three and a half years. He had started with water balloons in the first week of their freshman year. Billy did pester other students, but he particularly liked to pick on Amanda. It was never enough to get in serious trouble but enough to be very annoying. The worst was when he had filled the lock to Amanda's dorm room with chunky peanut butter. No one could ever pin the prank on Billy, but Amanda was sure that it was him.

After Billy disappeared, unfazed by her shout, she stooped down to pick up her books. "Oh no," she moaned. Her books were ok, only a little snow-covered. But her report was ruined; it had fallen in a slush puddle and was soaked. She tried to clean it up, but it still looked sad. "Better get going and see what Professor Kline wants me to do about this," she said to herself.

Amanda settled in her seat, turning her attention to the professor. "I hope that you all remembered to bring your reports today," Professor Kline began. "Remember, I told you that there would be a 25-point deduction for late work."

"Oh great," Amanda thought to herself.

"I will collect your reports and the end of today's

class. Today's topic is forgiveness." Professor Kline went on to remind them of Jesus' answer to the question: "How many times should I forgive someone?" He also talked about a parable that Jesus told about the wicked servant. In that parable, a servant was forgiven a huge debt by the king. Afterward, the servant threw some other servant in prison because he couldn't pay back what he'd borrowed. When the king found out, he was extremely angry and threw the wicked servant in jail. Professor Kline explained that forgiveness is one of Christianity's central themes.

At the end of class, he had the students come forward and hand in their reports. "I'm sorry, Amanda, I can't accept your report. I can't even read it," Professor Kline told her. The report had gotten wet enough that the typewriter ink had run.

"It wasn't my fault. I finished it last night. But on my way to class Billy Anderson knocked the books out of my hands. The report landed in a puddle," Amanda replied.

"It's ten o'clock now; I'll give you a twenty-four extension to turn it in. After that, I'll consider it to be late," Professor Kline offered. Amanda did some quick mental calculations. It was going to be next to impossible to get the report done on time, considering the rest of her workload. She considered another protest but decided against it. "Ok professor, thanks."

"I'll never forgive Billy Anderson for this," Amanda told her roommate Sara. "I have two finals tomorrow and another ten-page report for Advanced Anatomy. And now I need to retype this whole Christian Doctrine report. Arrrghhh."

"I feel for you, Amanda. I don't know how you're

going to get it done. I wish I could help, but I have three exams tomorrow that I have to cram for tonight," Sara said.

"Oh, I understand. I just don't know how I'm going to pull it off," she said.

Amanda worked most of the night typing reports and studying. She managed to get the papers finished and get three hours of sleep. But she didn't cram for the exams the way she had planned. Her first class the next morning was at 8:00; she got up at 7:45 and got ready as fast as she could. She ran across campus to face the first exam. It went awful; she had a hard time concentrating on the questions. Amanda was certain that she had failed it. 'I'll never forgive him," was her one recurring thought.

After the 8:00 class, she ran over to Professor Kline's office to drop off the retyped report. Professor Kline looked at his wall clock, 9:45. "Good, I'm glad you made it in time, thanks," he said as Amanda handed him the report. "Are you ok? You don't look like yourself."

"I'll be ok," she said. "I didn't get much sleep last night, all because of Billy," she said as she glanced at the clock. 'I've got to get going. Biochem starts in ten minutes." Amanda turned and began walking towards the door.

"Amanda, hold up a minute," Professor Kline said. Amanda stopped and turned. "What time is your last class over with today?" he asked.

"2:30, why?" she replied.

"I'd like to see you in my office after that and review some things with you, would that time work for you?"

"Sure, I guess," Amanda said. But her thoughts were, "Thanks, Billy, now you owe me a nap."

"Great, see you then," Professor Kline said. Amanda thought the request strange but hurried towards Biochemistry class.

—

"Amanda, I'm glad you could make it. Have a seat," Professor Kline said as he offered her a chair. Amanda's last class was another exam; it didn't go so well. "So, Amanda, how was your day?" asked Professor Kline.

"Awful, I had two finals today. I'm afraid I didn't do so well, thanks to Billy Anderson," she replied.

"That's one of the things I'd like to talk to you about. But first let me say that I already graded your report; it was very good." Professor Kline handed her report back to her. On the first page, Amanda took notice of the grade, an A-.

"Thank you, Professor Kline."

"That report tells me that you have a mental grasp of the material I presented in class. You should be glad that I don't grade on the application of the material. I'm afraid that you would receive a much lower grade." Professor Kline said.

"I'm not sure that I follow," Amanda said. "If you're trying to say I'm not a good Christian, well I don't understand. I'm faithful at church and chapel; I attend a couple of different small groups, try to read my Bible, and pray every day."

"Those are all good. What I'm talking about is putting the things you have learned into practice," he said.

"But I thought I was," she replied, still not grasping his meaning.

"Let me help you a bit," he paused, "Billy

Anderson?" Professor Kline said.

"What about Billy? Other than he's made my life miserable, especially the last 24 hours," she said.

"And what was yesterday's lecture about?"

Amanda thought for a moment. "I don't remember," she confessed.

"Does forgiveness ring a bell?" he asked.

"Yeah, that was it, but I still don't... oh you think that I should forgive Billy, is that it?" she asked.

"That is the general idea. I was hoping to get the two of you together this afternoon, but that didn't work out. Billy's last class was yesterday, and he won't be back," Professor Kline said.

Amanda smiled, "The College kicked him out?"

"No, he graduated mid-term," Professor Kline said. "But the question you just now asked says a lot about your attitude towards Billy. You thought the worst of him and relished the thought."

"So why are we having this conversation? I can't forgive him, so what's the use? Besides, I'll never see him again anyway because he lives in another state," Amanda said.

"We are having this talk for two reasons. The first is what the Bible says in Galatians 6:1. Brothers, if someone is caught in a sin, you who are spiritual should restore him gently. Whether you admit it or not Amanda unforgiveness is a sin. The second reason is... well let me ask you this question. You're in the nursing program, correct?"

"Yeah, so," Amanda replied

"What are you going to do if someday in the course of your job you need to provide care for Billy?"

"I'd ask someone else," she replied.

"Really? If he's lying on a gurney dying, you'd turn you back on him?"

"I don't know," Amanda said.

"AMANDA, I need you now!" screamed the doctor.

"I don't know," Amanda said to herself. "Wait a minute, yes I do. Lord Jesus, forgive me for carrying this load of unforgiveness and bitterness. Help me to help Billy and help me to forgive him. Amen." with that, Amanda sprinted down the hall to the ER room.

A few days later...

Amanda walked into Billy's room. "How are we today, Mr. Anderson?" she asked.

"Not bad considering. Hey, aren't you Amanda Patterson, OCC?" he asked.

"That's me, long time no see," Amanda said.

"I've been hoping that I'd run into you someday but not like this," Billy said.

"To be honest, I was hoping that I'd never see you again," Amanda replied.

"I deserve that. I was awful to you. Look, Amanda, I need to apologize for the way I treated you in college. Will you forgive me?" Billy asked.

"Professor Kline warned me a long time ago that this day might come. I had made up my mind to walk the other way if you ever came through the hospital doors. But when I read your driver's license and saw your name, God reminded me of a talk I had with Professor Kline. I forgive you; can you forgive me for hating you all these years?" Amanda asked.

"I think so," he said.

"One more, make that two more questions," Amanda said.

"Ok," he said.

"Why did you pick on me? And did you that put the chunky peanut butter in my lock?" Amanda said.

"I did do the peanut butter. Why I picked on you is harder to answer. I guess because I liked you. I know that that is not much of an answer," Billy said.

"You're right, that's not much of an answer. Maybe after you've laid there for a while you can come up with something better. And you are going to be here for a while. You're pretty beaten up from that accident," Amanda said. "By the way, I need to give you this shot. Can you roll over a little?"

"Are you sure you've forgiven me?" Billy asked.

"Let's find out shall we," Amanda said jokingly.

INSUFFICIENT FUNDS

Wisps of snow curl against the early morning dark as a beat-up green Chevy lurches to a stop. "600 hundred feet, you couldn't coast just a bit more?" A bundled figure complains slamming the door shut with a gloved hand. "Right there! That's all the farther you needed to go," the figure shouts at the silent car with a pointed the finger at a tall lighted gas-station sign. "Argh!" the figure exclaims walking away.

"I hear we're going to get six inches before its all said and done," a lanky truck driver says to the gal behind the counter of the gas station.

"Really? I heard one to three," she says while ringing up his coffee and donut.

"It all depends on the wind," injects another. "If we get the 20-30 mile an hour wind like they're saying it won't matter much either way."

"Thanks," the woman at the counter says

completing the truck driver's sale. "Have a nice day."

"You too," the trucker calls as he holds the door open for another customer.

"Me too what?" the bundled figure thought as he entered the brightness of the station. The figure pushes back his hood and unzips his coat revealing a young face with the start of a beard, blue jeans, and a decade-old faded t-shirt. "Well, Pete," the young face mumbles to himself, "where are the gas cans?"

Pete scans the aisles and spots them next to a small section of home hardware. He grabs one of the overpriced red-plastic containers and walks up to the counter.

"Morning Sunshine," the lady attendant says, "run out of gas or getting a jump on lawn mowing season?"

"Missed it by about 600 feet," Pete answers sliding his credit card through the reader. "Add a gallon of regular too."

"Sure will," the attendant says, punching in the order. "Well that's not good, try your card again." Pete slides it through. "Nope declined. Do you have another one?" Pete shakes his head no, rifles through his wallet and pulls out a debit card.

"Side that through and put in your pin," the attendant says. "Nope declined again. Any cash?"

Pete again looks in his wallet although he knows the answer already. "Sorry," he mumbles.

"Try the ATM, sometimes that works even when this thing declines someone," the attendant suggested. "You can just leave the gas can here until you get back."

Pete walks up to the ATM as if it might bite him. He slides in the card, punches in the pin numbers, and requests forty dollars. "Insufficient funds" the screen answers back. Pete tries again lowering his request to twenty dollars. "Insufficient funds" the unfeeling machine responds. "Once more, Pete," he whispers and punches in ten dollars. "Insufficient funds" the screen reports. Pete slams and kicks the machine in frustration.

"Hey, cut that out!" the attendant yells. "Frank, I need some help out here," she says into a microphone.

From a corner office, a short round man emerges. "What's up Marge?" Frank asks.

"See the guy in the blue parka? He's run out of gas and evidently out of money," Marge explains.

"I'll take care of him," Frank responds. All the while, Pete is staring at the ATM, hoping that it may somehow change its mind.

"Trouble, friend?" Frank asks, walking up to Pete. "Why don't you come over here and sit down," Frank says, pointing at two small tables in the back of the store. "I'll get you a cup of coffee, on the house." Pete nods and follows Frank to one of the tables. "What do you like in your coffee?"

"Just black," Pete mumbles as he sits staring at the red and white checked table-cloth.

"What's up, Frank?" a balding farmer in bib overalls and a red plaid shirt near the coffee counter asks.

"Yeah, what's all this ruckus," asks the banker in a pin-stripe suit next to him.

Frank leans over and whispers, "don't know the story, but it seems he's out of gas and out of money." Both men nod. "Listen guys, I'm really busy, think you could talk with him? See if there's someone he can call?" Frank asks. "I'd turn him out but with the snowstorm, well you know."

"Don't worry Frank, we'll talk to him," the farmer says.

"Thanks," Frank replied, "grab a medium-sized black coffee for him."

A few moments later, the farmer and the banker approached Pete with coffee in hand.

"Hi, Frank asked us to bring you this," the farmer says, handing over the warm cup. "I'm Ray, this here is Steve. What's your name?" Farmer Ray asks, pulling a chair over to Pete's table.

"Pete Scrimshaw," he says, taking a sip of the hot coffee.

"Where are you from Pete?" Steve asks.

"Lindsay Montanna, I doubt you've ever heard of it."

"So what are you doing clear over here by Fargo? Ray asks.

"I have a job offer in Duluth, a deckhand on a ship hauling grain to Ireland. It leaves tomorrow. Now, I'll miss it and the sign-on bonus that went with it."

"Surely they'll be other ships you could hire on with if you miss this one," Steve suggests.

"This is the last one scheduled out before the locks at Sault Ste. Marie close for the winter." Pete responds.

"Is there anyone you can call?" Ray asks. Pete shook his head. "No one?" Ray asks again.

"Hey, fellows, what's up?" bellows a tall man in mechanics overalls.

"Do you have anything of value? Perhaps we could

work something out?" the banker asks. "Car or anything I could use as collateral for a loan from the bank?"

"My car's worthless, maybe worth a few hundred. But it needs a few hundred more to fix the brakes and blown out muffler. About the only thing of value I have is this..." Pete reaches beneath his coat and pulls out a worn gold cased pocket watch. "I'm not sure what it's worth, it was my granddad's," Pete explains.

"Give you ten bucks for it," the tall mechanic offered having figured out what was going on.

"That's ridiculous Shorty" Ray countered.

"I won't sell it," Pete responds.

"Suit yourself, but you won't get a better offer," Shorty says. "Better decide quick, I need to push off. The sheriff called about a car stalled on 17, there's some old green Chevy he wants towed away so the snowplows can get by."

"That's my car!" Pete yells. "That's why I'm here, to get some gas and get going again."

"I'll loan you a hundred on the watch," Steve offers, throwing a green-tinted portrait of Franklin on the table.

"Well ain't that a fine how do you do," Shorty says. "Looks like you have some powerful new friends. I'll give you ten minutes. After that, I'm towing that ugly old car of yours to my lot, and it will cost you more than that 100 to get it back. I may end up with the pocket watch after all. I always wanted one."

"Come on, Pete," Ray says. "Take the loan and let's get that car moving."

A few minutes later, with filled gas can in hand all three pile into Ray's Silverado and raced to Pete's Chevy. It was quite the scene. While Shorty maneuvered his tow truck in front of the Chevy, Ray's truck pulled up behind. While the flashing lights of the Sheriff behind them painted the snow red and blue. All while Pete hurried to pour in the gas and get the car started.

"Sounds like you need to move that tow truck of yours," Ray said to Shorty once the Chevy came to life again.

"Can't win them all," Shorty responds with a kick of the Chevy's balding tires.

A few minutes later, Pete stood between the old Chevy and a gas pump watching the numbers tumble. "Well, this will be the shortest loan the bank ever made," Steve said, handing the pocket watch back to Pete.

Pete looked the watch over before sliding it into his pocket and reaching for his wallet. "I can't pay it all back, but here, take what's left," Pete said, offering the bills.

"Oh, no. You misunderstood. The loan is forgiven. It was worth it to see the look on Shorty's face. Besides, that pocket watch is more valuable to you than it would ever be for the bank or me. Take good care of it. Well, I need to get to work. Nice meeting you, Pete." Steve said.

As the banker walked away, Ray walked over. "Say, umm, I've been checking the weather and it's pretty ugly between here and Duluth. How about I give you a ride in the truck? It can bust through about anything and get you to the docks in plenty of time. My daughter lives over there so I can bunk with her until the roads clear up."

"What about my car?" Pete asks.

"Well, funny thing there. Before Shorty burst in, I was going to offer to buy it from you and give you a lift. I have a sixteen-year-old son it would be perfect for. Five hundred sound fair?" Ray offers.

"Deal," Pete says, offering to shake hands. "I was planning on selling it in Duluth anyway."

"Deal then," Ray confirms with a handshake. "My place is about three miles out. Follow me there, we'll finish up the paperwork and head out."

"Sounds good," Pete says, replacing the gas cap as a snowplow rumbled by on the highway.

"Have a nice day pump five," Marge calls over the intercom.

"You too!" Pete yells back.

Seasons of Forgiveness: Christmas

DANNY'S FIRETRUCK

Six-year-old Ben was the first to wake up that Christmas morning. He took a look to see if it was light out yet. Mom had been explicit last night, they couldn't get up until the sun was. "It must be light out," he thought, squinting to make out Winnie the Pooh watching from the dresser. Deciding it was ok, he jumped out of his bed. "Danny, wake up! It's Christmas," he said while giving his three-year-old brother a shake. In a few moments, Ben's excitement registered with Danny, and he was out of his bed in a flash.

Both boys sprinted down the hallway and burst into their parent's room. "It's Christmas," they yelled. Both boys ran back down the hallway towards the living room and their Christmas tree.

"Are you awake?" Rod asked Evelyn.

"Uh, barely, what time is it?" she asked.

"6:45," Rod said after checking the clock on the nightstand.

"I didn't know it was light this early," she said groggily as both began to stir out of bed.

The boys surrounded the tree, guarding the presents making sure none escaped. "Well boys why don't we wait until tonight to open these," Rod teased. The boys looked stricken. "Just teasing, Let me get some coffee on, and then once your mom's here, we'll see what's in all those packages."

This Christmas was going to be better for Rod's family than in previous years. Rod had only been in his new job for about 10 months. But they had managed to catch up on their bills, so there was a little extra available for Christmas. Not that Christmas was extravagant. Each boy received a new shirt and pants and one toy. Ben opened a set of building blocks while Danny got a bright red fire truck with a working ladder. "Woooooooo, wooooooooo," he mimicked, pushing it around the floor. Evelyn had also wrapped some candy bars and chewing gum to give the boys plenty of things to open. After all of the wrapping paper was picked up, Rod read the Christmas story out of the Gospel of Luke to them.

Next door, in Mrs. Anderson's house, the holiday was only noticed by the calendar. She had never had much family. What family she did have is too distant in relationship or geography to include her. She didn't mind though; she had a long habit of ignoring Christmas. Well, of ignoring everyone except when someone's grass grew a bit too long, or some trash cans lingered at the curb.

In the Parker's house on the other side of Rod's, Christmas wasn't missed, but gifts were few. Fred had been dreaming of a football since Thanksgiving, but his only present was a pair of jeans. Fred's father also had a new job, but with the recent medical bills from the newborn, their funds were very limited. Still, they celebrated Christmas as best they could. Fred really did have his heart set on a football.

After Christmas dinner, Ben and Danny went outside to play in the snow. Fred was already outside working on a snowman. "Hi Fred, Merry Christmas," Ben called.

"Merry Christmas, I guess," Fred replied while adding to his snowman's midsection.

"Whatcha get for Christmas?" Ben asked.

"A crumby pair of jeans, how about you guys?' Fred asked.

"We both got clothes too. Danny got a toy fire truck, and I got some building blocks."

"Wow, that's cool," Fred replied with a little envy.

"Fred, time to come in," his mother called.

"See you guys," Fred said, plodding back inside.

Danny pulled on Ben's coat to get his attention. "Fred no toys for kisstmas?" Danny asked.

"Guess not."

"Why?"

"You wouldn't understand; you're too little," Ben told him. "Let's go build a snowman."

"Otay," Danny replied.

After supper, Ben and his dad were playing with the building blocks while Mom cleaned up the kitchen. Mrs. Anderson, out on the sidewalk taking her Yorkie for a walk, noticed a small shadow sneak across Rod's yard. After her eyes adjusted a little more. She was able to make out a small coatless boy carrying what appeared to be a poorly wrapped present. Curious, she followed at a distance and spied as he snuck onto the Parker's front porch and placed his bundle by the front of the door. The little shadow then jumped up, pressed the doorbell, and sprinted back home.

Fred's mother opened the door and noticed the present. Taking a closer look, she could make out the lines of a toy fire truck through the holes in the wrapping paper. "Fred, come here," she yelled as Mrs. Anderson looked on from the sidewalk.

"Yeah, Mom?" Fred asked.

"I think that someone brought you something. Go ahead and open it." Fred removed the wrapping revealing a toy fire truck.

"Is this mine, Mommy?" Fred asked.

"I suppose so sweetie. Do you have any idea who could have left it?"

"Ben said that Danny got a fire truck for Christmas, but why would he leave it for me?"

From the sidewalk, Mrs. Anderson volunteered, "I don't know why, but I saw a small boy bring it over,"

"Oh," Fred's mom said. "I didn't see you there Mrs. Anderson. You saw Danny drop this off?"

"I was walking Sparky, and I saw a small boy come out of Rod's sneak over with a present and ring the bell," Mrs. Anderson said. "I don't know their names, but it was the littlest one."

"I wonder why?" Fred's mom asked.

"Why don't we go over to Rod's house and ask?" Mrs. Anderson suggested.

The four of them marched over to Rod's house: Fred with the fire truck, Fred's Mom, Mrs. Anderson, and Sparky. When they got to the front door, Mrs. Anderson rang the bell, which Evelyn answered.

"Mrs. Anderson, Fred, June, good evening. Can I help you?" she asked, puzzled by the delegation standing at her front door. Mrs. Anderson briefly explained the reason. "Why don't you come in and have a seat," Evelyn invited. And in they went, including Sparky who was ready to come in out of the cold.

Evelyn started by asking, "Danny, did you give Fred your fire truck?"

"Yes," he replied

"Why did you do that honey?" she asked.

"Fred sad, no kisstmas toy," he said.

"We couldn't afford much for Christmas this year," June offered shyly. "Hank started his new job a few months ago, and then the baby came. With the hospital bills, we didn't have enough money for much more than a pair of jeans. You know how little boys go through jeans."

"I sure do," Evelyn nodded. "We didn't have a much either. The boys each got some clothes and a toy; the fire truck was Danny's present."

"Fred, give the fire truck back to Danny," June said.

But before Fred could hand the fire truck back, Danny bolted out of the room. The adults sat and looked at each other, each one wondering what to do next. After a few moments, Mrs. Anderson softly said. "I've never seen anything like it. That little boy, he's, well, I've never seen a heart filled with that much goodness. Reminds me of something long forgotten." She grew introspective for a few moments. "It's been a long time since I've given anyone a Christmas greeting, would you mind?"

"Well no, Merry Christmas Mrs. Anderson," Rod said. They each, in turn, went around the small circle expressing their holiday greeting to her.

When it came back around to her, she said "Merry Christmas everyone. My, it's been a long time since I said that." The Yorkie gave a small yip as if to agree. From the next room a little voice joined in. "Merry Kisstmas Mrs. Anderson"

"I needed that," Mrs. Anderson said. A tear was rolling down one cheek. "Danny, come out here please I have an idea I'd like to share with you." Once Danny settled on his mom's lap, Mrs. Anderson continued, "Fred, do you like the fire truck?"

"Yea, I guess so," Fred said

"What did you really want for Christmas?" Mrs. Anderson asked.

"A football."

Mrs. Anderson turned to Danny. "If I get Fred a football for Christmas, will you take your fire truck back?" June started to protest, but Mrs. Anderson held her hand up.

"Otay," Danny answered.

"Ok, tomorrow Fred and I will walk down to Mr. Green's Store and pick out a football. If that is ok with you, Fred." He agreed and handed the fire truck back to Danny. "Now boys why don't you go play," she suggested. Ben and Fred scampered out of the room while Danny pushed his firetruck behind them going "Wooooo, Woooo."

"Thank you, Mrs. Anderson, you didn't need..." June started.

"Yes, I do. That little boy showed me what Christmas is all about, and I don't want any arguments. He reminded me it's about giving something of yourself and not expecting anything in return. It's been a long time since I've celebrated the season. I have some catching up to do." With that, she pulled the checkbook from her purse.

"Mrs. Anderson?" Rod started.

"Hush," she said sternly. Then she made out two checks. She handed one to Rod and the other to June. "I know that may seem like a lot of money. But, like Scrooge said, there's a lot of back payments included." With that, she pulled on Sparky's leash and rose to leave the room. "June, send Fred over at 9:30 tomorrow morning. Merry Christmas everyone," she smiled when she heard herself. "My, that feels good to say."

Mrs. Anderson kept her promises and more. A few months later, on a warm spring day, Rod looked out the living room window over at the park. He was surprised to see Mrs. Anderson pitching underhand to the boys while they took turns batting. When she saw Rod, she waved and mouthed, "Merry Christmas," and then returned to the game.

A PEARL OF FORGIVENESS

Pearl lives on the south edge of town in a sprawling two-room bungalow. Well, it seems sprawling to me because it's more than I have. Which is whatever open bed I can find at one of the downtown shelters. But this story isn't about me.

Pearl and I became friends back in High School. We were never lovers or anything like that, just friends. Through war, college, weddings, careers, and failures, we managed to keep track of each other. Now we're old and alone.

The one thing you need to know about Pearl is she is steady, her life ordered and predictable as she can make it. I'm part of that order I suppose although I share none of her desire to keep certain ducks in their place. On Thursdays, never on any other day, Pearl picks me up in her old Buick. I do whatever handyman kind of work she needs, she makes me a home-cooked supper and drops me off again at the shelter later that evening.

One day, after picking me up, Pearl took a different

route home. I noticed because it was a chink in her routine, a left-hand turn at the Kroger's instead of a right-hand one. "Pearl, you made a wrong turn," I pointed out.

"No, she moved," was her terse reply.

"Who moved?"

"Shannon."

Shannon is Pearl's only child. It was a rocky marriage that only managed to stay together with liberal quantities of Duct Tape and Superglue. And Shannon knew how to exploit each crack. In my day she would have been called a wild child, now they call them troubled. As far as I know, Pearl and Shannon haven't spoken in years. Their separation is not over one large thing. It's more like a mountain of pebbles. A multitude of small offenses piled on top of each other to the point they can no longer see each other.

"And how did you find out that she moved?" I asked.

"She wrote me a note" That's a first I thought.

"Did she say anything else in the note?"

I could see Pearl struggling to process her answer has she turned from Fourth to Belaire Drive. "There it is, her new place, the one with the candle in the window."

It was a simple tract home that looked like all the others around it. "Nice place," I said. "Why don't we stop and say hello?"

"No!" Pearl responded. I could tell that there was an earthquake in her soul. Her eyes were teary, but her mouth was hard, and her knuckles were white. "I don't want to talk about it. I need you to fix the sink again."

So, I fixed the sink, nothing much more than a

plugged trap. I fiddled with a few other things, but mostly we just talked like we always did with safe words and phrases. We each knew what doors we could open and which ones we couldn't. For instance, I never ask about her husband that died unexpectedly or the failed pension that was supposed to keep her comfortable. And Pearl knew to never, ever, talk about Vietnam and my time there.

"I need you to do one more thing," Pearl began. "There's a box in the attic with Christmas decorations, could you get it down?" Okay, that was another change in Pearl's world, she hadn't put up Christmas decorations since Frank died. It wasn't hard to find; the attic wasn't that big. And it wasn't difficult to bring it down, it wasn't a very large box. After brushing off the dust and cutting through the yellowed packing tape, we opened the box. Inside were a couple of old garlands, a string of lights, a few of boxes of Christmas ornaments, and an old electric candle. "Can you make sure the lights work?" Pearl asked after I had emptied the old box.

I tinkered with the lights until supper. Chasing down burnt-out bulbs on a string of Christmas lights is right up there with a root canal in my book, but it beats dumpster diving for pop cans. I even got that old plastic candle to work again after a bit of rewiring. The glow from that old candle seemed to make Pearl happy and sad at the same time.

After a home-cooked meal of sliced ham, baked sweet potato, and green beans, I began getting ready for the trip back to the shelter. "Here," Pearl said and thrust a piece of paper into my hand. "It's the note from Shannon." I scrutinized Pearl, this was opening one of those forbidden doors.

"You sure you want me to read it?" I asked.

"No, but I need someone to tell me what to do."

***

Merry Christmas Mom,

I know it's been a long time and some things have changed in me. I kind of feel like Scrooge on Christmas morning. I'm wondering if I could drop by on Christmas Eve. There're some things I need to say. But I don't want to barge in. Put a candle in the window Christmas Eve if you're ok with it.

Love, Shannon

***

"I don't know why you need my say so, put the candle in the window and have a sit down with Shannon," I suggested.

"I'm scared, I don't want it to end badly again. I don't think I could take it if it did," Pearl admitted.

I've never seen Pearl this way, she's always been a rock that nothing could touch. "Listen," I begin. "My social calendar isn't exactly full, so if you want me to be here, I can be. I know that Christmas Eve doesn't fall on a Thursday, but I can be here to help keep things from becoming a volcano. If you want me to that is."

Pearl nodded, "I don't know. Let's get you home."

I'd like to report that Christmas Eve was like a picture postcard with enough fluffy white snow to make everything look bright and clean. Instead, Pearl plowed through heavy, dirty slush as we headed towards her home. I was kind of surprised when she came around after lunch on a Tuesday, but I guess that she wanted someone there if

Shannon came over. Call me Switzerland! Oh well.

As we pulled into Pearl's drive, I noticed the electric candle glowing in the window. Its little light wasn't much, but it seemed to express extreme hope. Or is that me reading into the situation. Pearl set me to work decorating a sad little tree she had picked up at the Dollar Store while she began to work on supper.

The night seemed to come early, and the little candle in the window glowed even brighter. Shannon's note didn't say when she would drop by, so every noise and passing car got Pearl's attention and made her a bit more nervous. It wasn't long before a car did stop. A car door slammed shut. Footsteps discerned as they broke through the ice-crusted slush. A knock on the door. But Pearl didn't get up, she seemed frozen in place. Switzerland to the rescue.

I answered the knock and helped Shannon take off her coat like a proper butler would.

"You must be Shannon," I said. "My name is Buck, I help Pearl out every now and again."

"Nice to meet you," Shannon spoke with a little quiver. "Hi, Mom."

"Hi, Shannon," Pearl mumbled.

"Is it ok if I sit?" Shannon asked, pointing at a kitchen chair. "I was glad when I saw the candle in the window."

"I wasn't sure when... your note didn't say what time," Pearl began. "Or we would have had supper or something for you." The truth was that Pearl had made more than enough but had already put away the leftovers.

"That's ok. I ate before. I didn't want to put you out

or anything."

I could see that Pearl wanted to spit something back, but she held her tongue for once.

"Listen. Mom, I didn't want to cause you any trouble," Shannon began again. Oops, another landmine time for Switzerland to step in.

"It's no trouble at all, in fact, Pearl's been looking forward to you coming over all day. Isn't that right Pearl?"

"It is nice to see you, Shannon," Pearl agreed.

"Well, better get to it," Shannon whispered to herself. "Mom, I'm sorry for all the trouble I caused. Things have changed in my life, in me, and now. Well, now I know the hell I put you through. I only want to say I'm sorry, please forgive me. I, I really do miss you."

The moments between Shannon's plea and Pearl's response seemed to last forever. Like time itself was waiting for Pearl's words.

"It's not that easy," Pearl began with tight lips that bit her words. "You can't show up out of the blue, say a few words, and brush everything away."

Words soon boiled over as they lobbed long-stored accusations and past wrongs at each other. Soon they were both talking past each other with ever-increasing volume. Landmines, explosions, things weren't looking good. It felt as if they needed some UN Peacekeepers instead of Switzerland.

"SHUT UP," I bellow with the authority of a Drill Instructor. "Shut up, sit down, and cool down for a moment." Both women ease into their chairs. "Listen, you both have plenty of grievances to hurl at each other. But you have to find a way around them."

"That's well and good Buck, but..." Pearl began, but I cut her off.

"No! Don't start again." A vision flashed, maybe stirred by the fireworks between Pearl and Shannon. "Back in Nam, there was this guy, a jarhead like me, called Whitey. His real name was Blake Whitcomb or something like that. Anyway, he was a tunnel rat. The Vietcong had built this vast tunnel system to move men and supplies under our noses. Whitey's job was to dive into those dark booby-trapped tunnels and clean them out. One day Whitey dove into another tunnel. In the darkness, he heard the quiet footfall of someone moving around. He silently navigated the tunnel until he saw a shadow heading his way. Well, not really a shadow but a darker dark. He raised his Colt 45 and was about to pull the trigger when he heard "UuRah." He instinctively called back "Semper Fi." The shadow was another tunnel rat, another Marine that had entered from the other side. In the darkness, fearing an enemy, they almost shot one another."

"What's that got..." Shannon started.

"I'm not finished yet. At one level you two are at war, always have been, and it's hard to put all that aside. So, what you have to do is dig under the mountain of offenses you both built so that you can see each other again. It's unrealistic to think that you can magically forgive in a moment everything that has gone on. But you can push that aside for now. Not ignoring it but choosing to work through it as you can and to make friends with each other. Now, Shannon, I have a question."

"Ok, Buck, what is it?" Shannon replied.

"You said in your note and alluded to it a moment

ago that something changed in you. That something caused you to want to connect again with Pearl. What was it?"

Shannon took a deep breath, "I've found God. Tony and I have been going to church, learning about forgiveness and love. And while I've found happiness, I've also found a deep sadness about how I treated you, mom."

Pearl didn't say anything but slowly nodded as a tear ran down her cheek.

"I have an idea, at least for starters," I said. "How about if Shannon comes over for supper every Thursday? You can get to know one another again, tell each other about your week and stuff like that."

"As long as I can bring supper every now and again that would be great," Shannon added.

"Ok," Pearl agreed and in the spirit of the moment added, "Tell me about your church."

I can't report that everything was happy ever after. There were plenty of times when Switzerland stepped in to keep the peace. They did manage to whittle on the mountain some but never did get through it all. Within that first year, I got to know Shannon, her family, and her church. I even started going there myself, but that's another story.

DEWEY SPRINGS

The village of Dewey Springs is nestled somewhere between never mind and you're lost. There's a small cluster of buildings clad in aged wood and peeling paint. The centers of activity in Dew, as the locals call it, are the old Baptist Church, Brother's Hardware, and Bell's Diner.

On Sunday's, the church building boasts three services. The Baptist, the Congregational folks, and a group of Jesus People all time share the old building. I'm sure you could tell them apart if a group photo of them all existed. The straight-laced Baptist, the business casual Congregational, and the blue jean-clad Jesus People would be easy to find.

Where folks hang out the rest of the week depends on the time of day. Early morning and lunchtime folks gravitate towards Bell's Diner and their "World Famous Biscuits and Gravy." There's a good reason for this claim. It seems that one day some tourists from Germany got lost and ate at Bell's. They later sent a letter proclaiming the wonders of Bell's biscuits and gravy. That letter hangs in a frame by the cash register for everyone to see.

That leaves Brother's Hardware, which is the focal

point of the area the rest of the time. There are two mysteries about Brother's, both found in the name. No one knows or remembers why it is called Brother's. Hank Paulson has run the place for nearly forty years and is an only child. And it's actually more of a general store than what most folks call a hardware store. Brother's has hardware, groceries, a post office, animal feed, and other "got to have right now" things.

Nothing much ever changes in Dewey Springs. Sure, the seasons come and go. But even when Christmas time rolls around, there's little to mark its approach. Bell puts up a little greenery and places a candle in the window. Brother's adds a few Christmas items to their normal offerings. Each of the congregations put up their own Nativity scene around the old Baptist church. Folks do their own thing without much care for anyone else. But that's about to change.

One Saturday morning, few days before Christmas, a stranger walked into town up the road from Blue Eye. The morning was brisk and bright with a dusting of snow on the ground. Her raven hair was long and straight. The set of her brown eyes, the stride of her hiking boots, even her denim jeans and jacket all screamed purpose. Yet, she carried nothing else. No backpack, daypack, or those funny little pouches folks call fanny packs.

She beelined it to Bell's and took a stool at the counter. "How much for an order of Biscuits and gravy with some coffee?" She was overheard to say. "That much?" she replied to Bell. "Well, only some coffee then," she finally ordered.

"Where you headed to?" Bell asked as she sat down

the steaming cup.

"This here is Dewey Springs, right?" the stranger asked.

"Sure is," Bell nodded.

"Then I'm not headed anywhere but here," the stranger said between sips of coffee.

"Do you have folks here? Bell asked.

The stranger paused, "Well kind of, but not really. They're more like distant brothers and sisters." There was silence in the diner as the regulars tried to work that out.

"Well welcome to Dew either way," Bell said. "What's your name? Maybe we can help find your folks."

"You can call me Tiffany," the stranger replied.

There was one of those awkward pauses as everyone listened for Tiffany to reveal her family name, but she offered none. "And your folks are?" Bell trailed.

"They don't know me, but I'll know them," Tiffany replied as she finished her coffee and laid the right amount of money on the counter.

For the rest of the day, Tiffany wandered around Dewey Springs. She took her time strolling the aisles of Brother's Hardware, which made Hank nervous. She was seen looking over each of the nativities in the churchyard. For hours she sat on Dewey's Rock and studied the valley below. The town buzzed with wonder at who she was and why she was there.

At dusk, she entered the church while the Baptist choir rehearsed for the next day's service. The inside of the old building was warm and inviting. The worn benches spoke of years of service, while the overhead lights provided the right amount of soft glow. Tiffany found a spot in the back row and soaked in the choir's rendition of O Holy Night.

As the choir folks were leaving an older gentleman approached the stranger. "You must be Tiffany, I'm Pastor Martin."

Tiffany rose, "thank you for your service," she said as she shook the old pastor's hand.

"I was never in the...Oh you mean this," Pastor Martin said, pointing at his Bible. Tiffany smiled and nodded. "Well, you're welcome," he replied with a chuckle.

"Pastor," Tiffany began, "Would you mind if I stayed here tonight?"

"Well, if you have no place to go, you're welcome at the parsonage. We have a guest room."

"Thank you for your kindness, but if it is ok, I'd rather stay here. These old walls speak volumes to me. I can't think of a better place to be." Tiffany replied.

"Suit yourself," the Pastor replied. "Here are the lights, over there is the restroom. There's a kitchen in the basement if you're inclined to make coffee in the morning. Be sure you're up by 8:30 that's when the congregational folks show up, we have a go at 10:00 and the Jesus People start up at 1:00. If I recall right, they have a potluck at noon tomorrow if you're so inclined.

Sunday afternoon the gossip wires were buzzing across Dewey Springs. Tiffany stayed for all three of the services. Folks near her marveled at her clear and pure singing. She seemed to know all the words and melodies from the different congregations. Even the somewhat obscure modern tunes the Jesus People worship band offered.

What folks didn't see was her quiet invitation for each of the Pastors to meet her that evening on Dewey's Rock. Neither did any of the Pastor's share this odd request from the raven-haired stranger with anyone else.

In the cool dark of the night, hundreds of dots of lights blinked up from the valley as the stranger and the three pastor's gathered.

"Someone's been praying," Tiffany began.

"Well I hope so," quipped Dr. Strong of the Congregational church.

Tiffany giggled, "Let me be more specific. Someone's been praying for Dewey Springs and for you, for each of you."

"How would you know that?" Pastor Steve of the Jesus People wondered aloud.

"You wouldn't believe me if I told you," Tiffany replied. "But look here, how many lights do you see? Each one represents a household of what two, three, five, more?"

"Sounds about right," Pastor Martin confirmed.

"Over there, that one, right now a teenager is depressed about school. And that one," Tiffany pointed out a light on the opposite side of the valley. "A widow is lonely, forgotten, and without hope. Those are only a few of the folks down there falling between the cracks because you three are racing each other."

"No way!" exclaimed Pastor Steve. While Dr. Strong grimaced and Pastor Martin groaned. "How do you know all this!" Pastor Steve challenged.

"Sorry," Tiffany said. "I got ahead of myself. It's just that I see the wounds down there and the hope bottled up over there," she said, pointing at the church building.

127

"Dr. Strong, how many were at your service this morning?"

"45"

"Pastor Martin, what about your service?" Tiffany asked.

"58"

"Pastor Steve?"

"We don't count," He replied which earned him a silent stare from the others. "OK, about 28."

"I don't get it. So we know how many come to a service. What does that matter?' Pastor Martin asked.

"That's the problem, it's not how many come but how many don't, can't, or won't," Tiffany replied.

"So what do we do about it?" Dr. Strong asked. "We all do some kind of outreach. Pastor Martin's folks have a food pantry. Pastor Steve's crew often do give away garage sales. And we run regular encounter groups for different needs."

"And all that is very good, but it can be more," Tiffany replied.

"More what?" Pastor Steve asked.

"More of everything. By competing with each other, you are limiting yourself. What would happen if all three congregations supported each other's work? How many more could the food pantry feed? How much more could the clothing drive do? How many more could get the help and support they need to overcome their grief, addiction, or marriage problems? If you worked together, how much more could you do instead of what you're doing now?" Tiffany concluded.

The three pastors silently considered Tiffany's observation while the lights twinkled in the valley.

"In fact, let's do something tomorrow night," Tiffany suggested.

"Christmas Eve?" Dr. Strong asked.

"I know it's short notice and some folks will have family around, but sure. I'll take care of it. Just invite everyone to come at 5:30. Tell folks that I'm involved, the grapevine will take care of the rest. Oh, and ask everyone to bring something. Say exactly that, 'bring something.'"

The impromptu Christmas eve service was the talk of Bell's the next morning. No one was quite sure what to make of it, which stirred even more talk and curiosity. Folks talked as they watched Tiffany walk around the church, talking to no one in particular. Even more, as she waved her arms like she was putting up decorations or planning some event.

Around 5:30, folks began arriving. Tiffany put the pastor's to work sorting the various things people brought with them. On the east side, a pile of food was growing as folks brought items from their pantry. Christmas decorations folks brought found placed inside and outside of the church. Someone even brought a Christmas tree which found a home inside the door of the church.

Tiffany put Pastor Martin in charge of getting some folks dressed for the Christmas story. Pastor Steve gathered a band and choir from those willing. At 5:50, she chased everyone out of the building. At 5:59, she signaled for the church bell to ring three times. At 6:00, standing outside the church doors, she began singing "Joy to the World" which all heard and joined in.

At the close of the first verse, she opened the doors to the church and invited all inside. The old church hadn't seen a crowd that large since the day it opened.

With a nod from Tiffany, Pastor Steve kicked off a rousing, hand-clapping, foot-stomping rendition of Hark the Herald Angels Sing. Over the next 20 minutes, the band and choir worked its way through several of the classic carols. When the final strains of Away in the Manger drifted away, Tiffany stood. From the back of the church, a violin began playing Silent Night.

Without a script or Bible, Tiffany announced, "And it came to pass in those days, that there went out a decree from Caesar Augustus, that all the world should be taxed." As she recited the words, folks recruited from the audience acted out the parts.

The cast was mixed with old folks and young folks playing the parts in makeshift costumes. Pastor Martin's only concern was the angels. There weren't any, but Tiffany assured him that it would be taken care of.

Something wonderful happened when Tiffany recited, "And the angel said unto them, Fear not: for, behold, I bring you good tidings of great joy, which shall be to all people. For unto you is born this day in the city of David a Savior, which is Christ the Lord. And this shall be a sign unto you; Ye shall find the babe wrapped in swaddling clothes, lying in a manger." Tiffany seemed to grow as the words tumbled out. Some folks would later say that she seemed to glow as she spoke those words with closed eyes and uplifted face.

Then when Tiffany recited, "Glory to God in the highest, And on earth peace, Goodwill toward men.". Well, it seemed like the walls themselves reverberated with the voices of all the worshipers they had heard over their long years.

A moment later and all returned as it was. Tiffany continued the story and wove in the tale of the wise men.

Earlier in the evening, she insisted that each of the pastors play the parts of the wise men. Each did and brought boxes representing the gifts of gold, frankincense, and myrrh. As Tiffany spoke the last words of the Christmas story, the pastors turned and locked arms. The lights faded and candles were lit as the choir sang O Holy Night.

No one saw her leave. Their minds and hearts were all turned elsewhere. Nor did she ever return. But on the Christmas tree they found an angel perched on the very top where none had been before. The three pastors each wondered to themselves if they had just entertained an angel.

Folks have a hard time describing the changes in that old town nestled between never mind and you're lost. The old-timers gathered at Bell's Diner and Brother's Hardware know it. The folks in the valley feel it. And each Christmas-eve a tree topping angel sees it as folks gather in the old church to celebrate God's greatest gift.

ANGEL'S BREATH

"The Christmas Pageant will begin in five minutes," a nurse announces through the PA system. My daughter, Angel, has been typecast, beautifully and rightly so, as one of the Christmas angels. "Alright, let's see, wings?"

"Check," she replies.

"Golden thing that kind of sort of looks like a robe?"

"Check"

"Halo on straight?"

"Check, um I think?"

"What are your lines?"

"Daddy, I've been saying them all morning," she pleads.

"Come on, one more time."

"O that's terrible," she moans.

"You forgot your lines? That's ok the first one is..."

"No the TV," she says as she grabs the remote to turn up the volume. On the screen is a video of a manger scene without a Baby Jesus. The scrolling banner under the reporter proclaims, "Jesus missing from churches around the city."

"That's right, Mary Anne," the reporter begins. "Northside Presbyterian is the latest church to report that their Baby Jesus has been stolen. One week before Christmas and churches all over town are either taken down their Nativity displays or are bringing their Baby Jesus statuettes in at night. Police are clueless. Earlier today the Mayor of Greenville held a press conference imploring the thieves and pranksters to return the Baby Jesus." The scene cuts from the reporter to a sound bite from the press conference.

"That's hilarious," I say as I check the clock. "Better shut that off though, or we'll be late. Wig or no wig?" I ask.

Angel ponders for a moment, "No wig," she decides. "Do you have your phone so you can record it for Mom?"

"Check" I respond as I help her out of bed and maneuver the IV stand to her side. A shepherd in a wheelchair nearly runs us over as we leave the room. "I see that Charlie's excited about the play,"

"We all are," Angel observes. "We're finally doing something instead of having it done to us."

The hall by the nurse's station is set and darkened for effect. Pointing the camera at myself, I announce. "Um, Hi, ah welcome to St. Mark's Children's Hospital 2014 Christmas Pageant." I turn the camera back on the scene and mumble, "I hope this thing is recording." A tall fourteen-year-old boy stands stage left and begins...

"In those days Caesar Augustus issued a decree that a census should be taken of the entire Roman world. And everyone went to his own town to register. So Joseph also

134

went up from the town of Nazareth in Galilee to Judea, to Bethlehem the town of David, because he belonged to the house and line of David. He went there to register with Mary, who was pledged to be married to him and was expecting a child." (New Living Translation)

Another boy dressed in a brown robe pushes a wheelchair with a very pregnant looking Mary. The boy stops by a few of the nurses along the way to ask if there is a room in the inn. All smile and shake their heads. The boy then stops at a doctor and asks, "Any room, sir?" The Innkeeper doctor leans down, examines Mary with his stethoscope and effects a worried look.

"You'd better get her indoors, I don't have any rooms, but you can use the stable," the doctor reports as he points the way. The tall boy continues,

"While they were there, the time came for the baby to be born, and she gave birth to her firstborn, a son. She wrapped him in cloths and placed him in a manger because there was no room for them in the inn."

Mary and Joseph disappear into an examine room. One of the nurses squeezes a toy which plays the same lullaby used when the hospital announces a birth. The couple reappears with a baby doll and settle in while four wheelchair rolling shepherds appear.

"And there were shepherds living out in the fields nearby, keeping watch over their flocks at night. An angel of the Lord appeared to them, and the glory of the Lord shone around them, and they were terrified."

Three angels, one of them my Angel, step in front of the shepherds. Two security guards illuminate the angels with their flashlights from across the room. "Fear not," my

Angel says. "We bring you good news of great joy," announces the second angel. "For today in Bethlehem the Savior, Christ the Lord, has been born," proclaims the third angel. "You will find the baby lying in a manager," my Angel says. Together they say, "Glory to God in the highest, peace and goodwill toward men." The angels retreat, and the security guards lower their flashlights.

"Let's go see this thing," one of the shepherds encourages. The others nod in agreement and spin towards Joseph and Mary.

"So they hurried off and found Mary and Joseph, and the baby, who was lying in the manger."

"Slow down," one of the nurses whispers as the shepherds speed by.

"When they had seen him," the boy narrator continues, "they spread the word concerning what had been told them about this child, and all who heard it were amazed at what the shepherds said to them. But Mary treasured up all these things and pondered them in her heart. The shepherds returned, glorifying and praising God for all the things they had heard and seen, which were just as they had been told."

After the shepherds retreat, aids dressed like camels push three wheelchair-bound kings into view.

"After Jesus was born in Bethlehem in Judea, during the time of King Herod, Magi from the east came to Jerusalem and asked, "Where is the one who has been born king of the Jews? We saw his star in the east and have come to worship him. King Herod suggested that they search in Bethlehem after a scribe recalled a prophecy concerning the City of David. After they had heard the king, they went on their way, and the star they had seen in the east went ahead of them until it stopped over the place where the child was." The security guards focus their flashlights on the ceiling above Mary, Joseph, and the baby. "When they saw the star, they were overjoyed. On coming to the house, they saw the child with his mother Mary, and they bowed down and worshiped him.

The camels push the kings closer. "We have gifts for the baby, mine is gold." The first king offers Joseph a bedpan filled with gold foil-wrapped chocolates. "Mine is frankincense" the second king offers holding out a spit tray filled with cotton balls. "Here, have some Myrrh, whatever that is," suggests the third king holding out a urinal with a pale golden liquid. Joseph tentatively grabs the container. "It's not what it looks like" the third king loudly whispers, "Its Mountain Dew." The crowd chuckles at this unexpected departure from the script.

After the Kings leave the head nurse claps her hands and announces, "OK children, gather around like we practiced." All the cast members make their way forward and sing Joy to the World. As the song ends the audience of family, friends, and hospital staff shower them with a healthy round of applause. Once things quiet again, the head nurse announces, "Thank you all for coming. I know that it means a lot to our children. There are refreshments in the waiting room. Merry Christmas to all."

Turning the camera back on myself, I say, "Merry Christmas." Then blurting out I yell, "Hey, would anyone mind if I uploaded this to YouTube?"

The next day my wife and I are standing by Angel's

bed as a doctor examines her.

"You did very well in the play yesterday, you were a wonderful angel." the Doctor says while he listens to her breathing. "Ok, you can lay back down. How are you feeling?"

"Tired, I suppose. Some pain, like a 5, right here." Angels said while pointing to her side below the rib cage.

The Doctor makes a note, "We'll get you a little something for that. The nurse will take care of you while I talk to your Mom and Dad. Okay?" Angel nods and closes her eyes. The Doctor signals us to follow and leads us to one of the small conference rooms. "Angel's cancer has reignited, and it's spreading faster than ever," the Doctor calmly says. "You have some decisions to make, I'm afraid that there is nothing more we can do."

"How long until, um?" my wife asks without looking up.

"Well, that's one of the decisions. If we do nothing, she has a week at the most. We could do some very heavy chemo and maybe buy a couple more weeks. But she's weak and barely recovered from the last round. I'm afraid that her quality of life during those extra few days would be poor and painful. But it is your decision. We also need to talk about end of life care."

"But she's doing better, you saw her yesterday at the play!" I argue.

The Doctor pauses. "Yes, she had a good day yesterday, but that was her body reacting to the chemo leaving her system. It's like a runner training with weights, take off the weights, and you feel as light as a feather for a bit. Her weakness is already catching up to her, you saw that today." The Doctor looks at both of us, "I'll leave you alone to discuss this. Would you like me to call the Chaplain?"

My wife nods yes while I shake my head no. The Doctor purses his lips for a moment, "I'll call him anyway, at least he can sit with you and maybe answer some of the procedural questions."

My wife and I look at each other. Tears roll down her cheeks while I stiffen and clench my fists in fear and anger at what lies ahead.

I'm not happy about it, but I lost the fight. I would have rather stayed at the hospital and fought the cancer until the last moment. Angel and my wife decided differently. The hospice counselor keeps talking about the stages of grief, I guess I'm stuck at anger while they've moved on to acceptance.

Christmas morning should be a time of wonder and magic. Mine is filled with anger, dread, and frustration. They've got Angel so pumped with morphine that she's out of it most of the time. Instead of the buzz of family and friends enjoying each others company, we are a muted and somber bunch. Someone has turned on the TV, which is running the annual marathon of "A Christmas Story." The silliness of Ralphie's desire for the "Red Ryder BB Gun" is bitter irony given my sole desire to have my Angel well again. I stare at the screen like a zombie, fruitlessly trying to escape into the silliness of Ralphie's dilemma.

"Dear, Angel's awake." my wife says, pulling me back to reality. Hand in hand, we walk to her room. The hospice nurse moves aside as we approach Angel's bedside.

Catching my eye, the nurse slowly shakes her head and mouths, "not long now."

Gently taking Angel's hand, I lean down and say, "Hi honey."

"Hi, Dad," she whispers.

"You were so cute in that play," I begin struggling to find something good to talk about. "Our YouTube video has over 20,000 views, what do you think about that?"

"That's nice Dad," she manages as she fades for a moment. "Dad, fear not. Find the baby lying in the manger," she whispers and fades, never to return.

"She's gone," the Hospice nurse confirms.

Hugs and cell phones become the order of the day as those gathered offer us shallow comfort and make the obligatory phone calls. I hang in there as long I as can stand it, which isn't long. There is no comfort for me, only a smothering, smoldering burn that needed fresh air to become a flame. So I escaped. I walked out. My neighbor Phil tries to follow, determined that shouldn't be alone until I threaten to give him a black eye for Christmas.

Alone I wander the streets, angry at God, angry at the world, the doctors, the well-wishers, and at Christmas. My wandering takes me past a large stone church with a tall steeple. As I pass their Nativity display, I notice that there is no baby in the manger. "I wonder if the thieves took him or if he's safely hiding inside," I mumble. The church bells ring 10 o'clock and begin a rendition of Joy to the World. My anger and the bell's joy fight for a few moments until Angel's last words echo in my head, "find the baby lying in the manger."

I hurry to the corner and turn right, there's another

church a few blocks ahead. Their Creche is beside their white framed entrance, but baby Jesus is AWOL. I visit church after church with no luck, the bandits have done their jobs well. While crossing the downtown district to continue my search on the other side of town, I stumble across a storefront church. I had never noticed it before. Plywood versions of the stable, Mary, Joseph, and the rest of the cast are attached to the building. Resting on the sidewalk in front of Mary and Joseph is a small wooden manger complete with baby Jesus. Lifting the doll from the manger, I cradle it and walk to their door.

"New Life Chapel, Rev. Josiah Brining," the door proclaims. I push against the door expecting it to find it locked, but it swings open. "Hello! Anyone here?" There is no foyer. Instead, I see rows of folding chairs under a low ceiling. The room is dark except for some Christmas lights decorating a small stage. Scattered about are the remainders of a Christmas pageant. I see movement in the deep shadows to the right of the stage. "Hello, Sorry to bother you. You, um, left your baby Jesus out last night." Out of the shadows steps an older black gentleman with short-cropped salt and pepper hair.

"Just a moment. Let me get the lights," he says, walking to the left side of the stage. In an instant, the room is flooded with light. "There, that's better. I wasn't expecting any company this morning," he explains as he walks my way. "I'm Reverend Brining, but folks call me Josiah."

"Hi, um, I'm Dan Carter. You left your baby Jesus out last night. I thought you might want it so the pranksters don't steal it." I say holding out the wrapped doll out to him.

He begins to chuckle. "We want them to take it," he explains. "Unwrap the doll." Doing so, I notice that a taped envelope around the baby's midsection. "In that envelope is a letter inviting them to church and a twenty-dollar bill."

"But why?"

"Jesus told us to give our shirts to those that steal our coats, this is our way of fulfilling that command. Why don't we sit," Josiah offers and moves some of the chairs around so we can see each other. "That's better," the old pastor sighs. "Now, I see that you're troubled about something deeper than someone stealing a doll. What's going on?"

"I've lost my Angel," I respond while looking at my shoes.

"They've stolen your angel?"

"No, my daughter, she, um, passed away this morning. She has cancer."

"I'm sorry," Josiah softly replies. "It's never a good day to lose someone, but Christmas day, that's hard. How old was she?"

"She's eight."

"Does your family, your wife know you're here? I mean, you should be with them."

"I got so angry that I had to get away and get alone." I go on to relay Angel's last words and my search for a baby Jesus lying in a manger. "My wife, she, well she, oh my. Can I borrow a phone?" Josiah pulls a cellphone from his pocket and hands it to me.

"Hello, this is the Carter's," an unfamiliar voice says.

"Hi, hey this is Dan can you put Doris on?" In the background I hear, "Hey Doris, its Dan, we've found him." A few moments later, I hear the ruffle as the phone passes to Doris.

"Dan?! Are you alright? Where did you go?" My wife asks.

"Doris, I'm sorry. I had to get out of there. I'm downtown at a church. Did you know there's a church next to Wallace Jewelry?"

"I called the cops, they're looking for you. How soon are you coming...Your downtown, how'd you get...? Oh, never mind, how soon are you coming home?"

"I can give you a ride," Josiah offers.

"Soon, ten minutes or so," I suggest. "Please call the police and tell them that everything is ok. I'll see you soon, love you."

"Ok, hurry back, I need you." she pleads. I hand the phone back to Josiah, "thanks for offering to give me a ride, we live up in Wildbrook, are you sure that's ok? Anyone, you need to call?"

"No, I'm by myself now. My Betsy died a few months ago, pancreatic cancer. This is my first Christmas alone. I was angry like you when God took her. Angry with the doctors, angry with the world, angry with God."

"But you're a Reverend..." I begin.

"And a person, like you," he corrects.

"So how did you get over it, the anger part?" I ask, hoping to find a way out of this dark place.

"What I tell folks is that you can't beat it out, burn it out, or drink it out you can only forgive it out." He pauses, "I didn't realize how true that was until Evelyn died. I had

143

to forgive the doctors, the world, and most of all, God. What I didn't realize is that I also needed to forgive myself. Say why don't we get you home, give me a moment to lock up." While Josiah was shutting off the lights, I wander back outside and place the baby back in the manger.

"So how can you forgive like that?" I ask after Josiah's battered Buick had left the curb.

"You were holding the answer in your arms, that's what your little girl was trying to tell you. Jesus is the only way we can forgive so deeply and completely. Look at all those decorations." He says as we pass through town. "Christmas is all about God becoming human, becoming flesh and blood like you and me. But Christ's mission was to provide forgiveness for mankind. Remember what the angels announced? 'we bring you good news of great joy for everyone' and 'peace on earth,' right?"

I thought back to Angel's play at the hospital, "Yes."

"Well, Jesus also wants to come and live in our hearts, our soul. By receiving his forgiveness, we can forgive others, by receiving his love, we can love others. Today can be a whole other kind of Christmas for you. Left or right here?"

"Um, left," I reply. Between giving directions, I accepted Josiah's offer. I forgave everyone on my list, including God and myself. I asked God for forgiveness and for His direction. With each word, I felt more of the anger melt away. "I don't feel as angry anymore..." I reported.

"Good," Josiah encourages.

"But I feel empty and sad," I continue.

"That's normal everyday grief, you will always have

that although the pain of it will lessen. I still feel that way myself sometimes. Today is one of those times." Josiah confessed.

"It's the third house," I instruct after we turn on Cedar Street.

"You mean the one with all the cars in front?" Josiah asked.

"Sorry, I guess that was a bit obvious. Will you come in? I'd love for you to meet Doris?" Josiah nods, and he parks the car a few doors down.

INTERVIEW WITH A SHEPHERD

-The Reporter-

One morning I was sniffing around the Jerusalem market, not for spoiled artichokes but for a story. Somewhere between Persian spices and dead chickens, I ran into Denny, one of my favorite sources. Denny was just a nickname, one he picked up because of his annoying coin flipping habit. "Denny, whatcha been up too?"

"You know I hate that name Squint," he said in retaliation. Taking out a denarius, he began to flip it in the air, "I've just come up from Egypt, traded a load of Galilean dried fish for some spun cotton."

"Pick up any news? My editor is about to fire me if I don't come up with something good."

"Pretty straight trip, roads were busy because of the crazy census. Even had to sleep under the stars one night, the inns being full and all. Now there's a story for you, price gouging in the wake of the census by highway innkeepers. The headline could be something like – Innkeepers the New Highway Robbers?! Watcha think?"

147

Denny smiled, trying to sell me on the story.

"Naw, my editor's uncle runs an inn in Bethlehem, he'd never go for it."

"Bethlehem, I hate that place it always stinks of sheep. You know I wasn't the only one trying to sleep under the stars." Denny said still trying to sell me the Innkeeper story. "There was this caravan from Persia, strangest thing I ever saw."

"What?" I encouraged.

"Well, they weren't selling anything. No trade goods at all. More like they were going to some royal gathering. I'd hope to trade with them before they came to the market, you know get a good deal, but they didn't have anything or want anything. Well..." Denny thought for a moment, "that's not true."

"Come on, what did they want?"

"Information, they wanted to know where the king was born." Strange I thought, wanting to see a king's birthplace. "Anyway, I told them to head south to Edom. Perhaps someone down there knows where Herod was born. Turns out that they weren't looking for Herod's birthplace but some new king. They even had gifts for the baby."

"Running a story like that wouldn't get me fired, it would get me killed. You know how jealous King Herod is." In my annoyance, I snatched Denny's coin in mid-flight. "Come on, Denny, you always see something worth writing about out there. Think! Anything strange, anything out of place? Egypt, Beersheba, Debir, Hebron, Tekoa, Bethlehem. You went through all of those places there has to be something." My annoyance turning to desperation.

"Bethlehem, there was something strange going on there."

"What?"

"I don't know. I had to camp out to the west of town. The Innkeeper wanted to triple the average rate. I really think you should run with that story."

"Forget the price gouging story, what happened in Bethlehem?"

"Okay," Denny paused for a moment composing his tale. "I was just about asleep when I heard several people running through my campsite. Looking out the tent flap, I saw a group of shepherds running towards town. When I stepped out to get a better look at the commotion, an older shepherd ran into me. 'Whoa, what's up friend?' I asked. Well, the old boy just stammered and pulled away. All I could get out of him was 'angels.' Wondering what had startled them, I sent a servant backtrack the way they came and returned to my hard bed. The next morning the servant reported finding a shepherdless flock of sheep. He stayed with them for a watch and quietly left when the shepherds returned."

"That's your strange thing, a bunch of drunk shepherds?" I asked incredulously.

"No, that's just it. The old shepherd wasn't drunk, I didn't smell it on him. Although the sheep smell was a bit overpowering. Anyway, whoever heard of shepherds abandoning their flock and running into town where everyone would see them?"

I thought about Denny's suggestion. It might work. Anything with angels would stir controversy between the Pharisees who believe in angels and the Sadducees who don't. And as my editor always says – "controversy sells." Slapping Denny's coin back into his hand, I explain my angle.

"It might work, but I think the innkeeper story is better," he observed.

"You never give up," I retorted.

-Bethlehem-

It took a bit of fast-talking to convince my editor to let me pursue the lead in Bethlehem. Two things were in my favor; the news desk was slow, and I could stay at his uncle's inn for free. Finally, he agreed. Giving me a letter for his Uncle Levi and a few coins for expenses he sent me on my way.

Bethlehem was still bustling with travelers when I arrived, much different than my last visit. I had stopped by on my way to Debir to chase down a lead about the olive crop failure. Bethlehem was quiet then, almost drowsy. It was more like Jerusalem on market day the day I began my search for the shepherd. With the letter in hand, I approached Uncle Levi's inn and gave the door a few quick raps. After a few minutes, I heard a gruff, "No Room."

"It's Nate from the Jerusalem Journal, Benjamin sent me," I yelled through the door. After a few moments, I heard the bar being raised and the door creak open.

"Nate! Out traveling again for my nephew? Come in," the old innkeeper invited. "Let's see, your last visit was what, three months ago?"

"Something like that. Nice to see you again."

"So where are you off to this time? Egypt, perhaps?" Levi asked.

"No, I'm following a lead right here in Bethlehem." Levi's eyebrows arched a bit wondering what story could be found in his village. I handed him the letter which he immediately read.

"So my Benjamin wants me to put you up as a favor, feed you too I suppose. How long are you planning on staying?"

"Only a day or two, it shouldn't be hard to find one shepherd."

"It might be harder than you think, there are many shepherds, and they are all scattered about in the hills." Levi thought for a moment before continuing. "Tonight you'll have to sleep on the floor. Tomorrow will be another story, but you are welcome to stay for as long as you need. Since you won't be paying in denarii you'll have to pay me in news, supper is ready, come and tell me what is going on in the big city."

As requested, I told Levi all the news that I could come up with. He took great interest in court gossip and asked if there had been any unique visitors. Since that wasn't my beat, I couldn't answer him. Eventually, the conversation came around to why I was at his table.

"So what's this about a shepherd? Expecting a drought of Passover lambs?" Levi asked.

"Nothing like that this time. A trader called Denny told me about something that happened the last time he passed through."

"Denny? Who's Denny?"

"Oh, that's my nickname for him. His real name is

David Ben Aaron. I call him Denny because he is always flipping a denarius." Levi's eyes reflected remembrance when I mentioned Denny's habit.

"He's a rascal Nate, I wouldn't give a copper mite for anything that he says."

"Well, he told me that a few days ago when he was in town..." I went on the relay Denny's story about meeting the shepherd and the report of angels.

"Yes, that was a very busy and strange night," Levi remembered. "We were full up, I had to turn a dozen or so away including your friend. There was one couple that I took pity on. They had traveled from Nazareth because of the census. She was soon to give birth, maybe a little sooner than they expected. Anyway, the inn was full, but I couldn't turn them out into the cold like I did to your friend. My stable boy suggested that we could clear out a stall for them. With my approval, he quickly moved the cows, mucked out the stall, and laid down some fresh straw. The young woman's birth pains began soon after they were settled. She is the fifth, no sixth, to give birth at my inn, although she is the first to do so in the stable."

"I can think of worst places." I thought there may be a human interest story worth looking into. "What did she have?"

"A lovely baby boy. But that's not the strange part. The next morning I visited the new family to assure them there would be a room for them later that day. Joseph, the new father, informed me that more shepherds may come to visit the infant. It seems that a group came out of the hills, and more may do the same." Levi looked at me and shrugged. "Who am I to argue with a new father?"

"So that was probably the shepherds that Denny saw," I reasoned. "Did Joseph say anything about how the shepherds knew about the baby?"

"I asked him that very question. 'God must have told them,' was all he would say." Levi rose and began clearing the table. "It's getting late Nate, give me a few minutes to make up a mat. You'll be warm at least, we can talk more in the morning.

I was tired but had one question I had to get out of the way. "Say, Denny told me you raised your rates because of the census. Anything to that?"

"What exactly did that weasel tell you?" Levi quickly asked.

"That you wanted to charge him three times the expected rate."

"I warned you not to trust him, the truth is the exact opposite. We were full when he arrived, he offered to pay me three times over if I would kick someone out so he could have a room. I told him no."

I knew Denny's story was a non-starter, but there seemed to be plenty of others to investigate.

-The Stable-

The next morning Levi introduced me to his stable boy. "Perhaps Dan can tell you more about the shepherds," Levi said by way of introduction. Dan was only about thirteen or fourteen and a bit tall for his age.

"Want to see the stable?" Dan asked, enthusiastically.

In my mind, if you've seen one stable, you've seen

them all. "Sure, why not," I replied. Dan's stable was an opening in the rocky hillside, primarily a cave that had been adapted for its purpose. Walls of stone and mortar separated the various stalls. And yes, it did smell like a stable; pungent manure mixing with dried straw, sweet hay, and dusty animals. All in all, though, it was cleaner than most I'd been in.

"This is where they had the baby," Dan said, pointing out a space near the rear of the cave. The stall was still empty, the straw looked like a nest around where the family had slept. Carved in the back wall was a shelf of stone with a rounded bottom, a kind of manger for the cows to eat from. In the manger was a smaller nest of straw.

"So tell me about that night."

"Well for most of the night I was putting up guest's animals, the stable was overflowing between our milk cows and the assorted horses and donkeys of travelers. When I went to report to Levi that I had finished the chores, I found him talking with some travelers. I overheard Levi turn them down, but I could tell his heart wasn't in it. Seeing the woman's condition, I suggested that we could move the cows and make up a place in their stall. The couple agreed, and Levi sent me off to get everything ready. When Mary entered the stable, she doubled over and moaned. I thought she disliked the smell, but the husband, Joseph, sent me to find the midwives. I spent the rest of the evening running errands for them, getting water, towels, and such. After the birth, I ran to the inn to give Levi the good news. He asked me to see if the family wanted anything to eat. When I returned, the midwives had gone, and the mother was suckling the newborn. I asked about getting them some food, Joseph thought some bread and a little cheese would be nice. As I was leaving a group of shepherds came striding towards the stable entrance."

"Did they say anything?" I asked.

"They only wanted to know where the baby was. I pointed to the stall and left to fetch Joseph's request. By the time I got back, the shepherds were all gone except the oldest one. 'Thank you so much,' I heard Joseph say. 'We will treasure your words and tend this little one as you suggest.' With that, the shepherd left."

"That's it? Did you know any of them? Did you hear them say anything about angels?"

"They were all from Judah's flock. The last to leave was old Samuel, their head shepherd."

"Any idea where they might be?"

"Like all the flocks, they keep to the hills. Who knows where they are at right now. You asked about angels, I didn't hear the shepherds say anything, but I did ask Joseph how the shepherds knew they had a baby. He said that the angels told them.

"Do you know if Mary and Joseph are still in town?"

"They left the night before last after the kings came to visit. Joseph said something about not being safe. I'm not sure what he meant, what could be safer than Bethlehem?"

I was disappointed I had missed the young family. But I was curious about Dan's mention of kings, surely Herod had not been here. I questioned him about it, but he clammed up and suggested I ask Levi. The rest of my day was spent fruitlessly roaming the hills in search of the shepherds.

-The Magi-

"Good morning, Nate, breakfast is ready," Levi
called from the hallway. I moaned as I lifted the blanket.
Yesterday's search had only yielded achy muscles. The
consensus of the shepherds I did find was that Samuel had
moved his flock further south.

"Alright, I'll be right out," I yelled back.

Eating breakfast in the great room was like a
geography lesson. I had fun guessing where each traveler
was from and where they were heading. With the census
still underway it's a bit more challenging given the similar
dress and appearance of those from Israel. After Levi had
seen to the needs of his other guests, he came by to enquire
about my search. It didn't take long to fill him in.

"The hills to the south are more rugged, perhaps
you should borrow one of the donkeys. I'll have Dan get
one ready for you," Levi decided, leaving to find the stable
hand. Alone with my thoughts, I tried to assemble the basic
storylines I had come across. Three stood out, the baby
born in a stable because of the census, the angel sighting
shepherds, and the mysterious kings. I decided to corner
Levi about the kings when he returned.

"Dan will have a donkey ready in a few minutes,"
Levi reported when he returned.

"Thanks, Levi," I replied although I wasn't too sure
about the idea of bouncing over the Judean hillsides, but it
was better than walking. "Say, I've heard bits and pieces
about some kings coming to Bethlehem, but no one has told
me the story, what do you know?"

Levi paused, weighing the request. Leaning forward, he whispered, "I'll tell you what I know if you promise to never publish the story."

"What! Why?"

"Because the baby's life is at stake, Herod will kill the child if he finds him."

"Can I publish something after the child is safe?" I implored.

Levi again weighed the issue. "If you promise to hold the story until the child is safe from Herod then I agree."

"I promise by heaven to hold the story until then," I solemnly spoke.

Levi leaned back, "First of all, the caravan was not of kings but magi. They came from the east, probably Persia."

"Magi? What are they?"

"If you are going to be a good reporter, you'll need to expand your knowledge outside of Jerusalem and Rome. Magi are a group of learned men, kind of like our priests. However, instead of seeking God in the Holy scriptures, they look to the stars. Something they saw in the sky led them here, to this very house."

"Did you speak to them? How did they know to come here? Where did they go?"

"So many questions. Yes, I spoke briefly with one of them. It appears that they started their journey many months ago. Their observations of the stars led them to believe that a royal birth was about to take place in Judea. So they came west expecting the birth to be heralded and, therefore, easy to find. Eventually, they enquired at Herod's court. However, even King Herod was surprised by their news. He summoned the High Priest and scribes to court. 'Where is the Messiah to be born?' He demanded the priests. They replied that according to the prophet Micah, it was to be in Bethlehem. Herod asked the magi a few more questions and sent them on their way to find the baby."

"I'm surprised Herod didn't lock them up."

"Herod's too much of a fox for that. Instead, he'll use the magi to find the child and then deal with the threat as he did with his own sons."

I grimaced recalling how Herod had recently executed several of his sons. "Let's talk about something better, when did the magi come and how did they find the baby?"

"They came the evening after the birth. By then, we had moved the family from the stable and into a room. Shortly after supper, there was a knock. 'No room,' I replied. Someone answered that they were looking for the baby. I expected to find another group of shepherds or other well-wishers when I opened the door. Instead, I was confronted with a royal court. 'Pardon the interruption,' one of them said. 'The star guided us here,' said another. 'May we see the child?' Asked the third. Knowing that Joseph and Mary's room was too small for such a visit, I asked the magi to wait in the courtyard while I prepared a place. We quickly cleared the great room and created a reception area. I told the family what was happening and invited them down to the hall. Joseph asked a few questions and then decided it would be okay. Once they were settled, I opened the door and invited the magi to come in."

At that moment, Dan burst into the great room and

announced that my donkey was ready.

-The Gifts-

Now, what do I do? Levi's half-way through his story about the magi and the donkey's ready for my shepherd search. "The donkey can wait," suggested Levi. I thought for a second and remembered my editor's advice, "never interrupt a man that's talking."

"Alright, let's finish the story," I agreed.

"Each of the Magi carried a small chest as they walked in," Levi began without noticing that Dan had joined us at the table. "For a few moments, they stood and admired the baby cradled in Mary's arms. Then one of them, the oldest one I think, began to explain their presence."

'We have come from a far off place in search of the newborn king of Judea. The heavens foretold his coming, and a star led us to this very house.'

'We are told,' began another, 'that your scriptures prophesy concerning his birth, and that the baby is more than a king – He is the Messiah of God.'

'Therefore, we have sought the child to worship the newly born king and Messiah.' explained the third magi. "At this point, each knelt before the family," continued Levi. "It was a strange and awesome sight. The magi in fine silks, bright sashes, and tall turbans kneeling before a poor family from Nazareth dressed in dull homespun."

"Tell him about the chests," Dan encouraged.

"I'm getting to that," Levi replied momentarily distracted by Dan's presence. "The older one spoke next.

159

'We bring gifts for the child from our homeland to honor and bless him, gold.' The older magi opened a small chest filled with gold coins. 'Frankincense,' the middle magi announced. The sweet aroma of frankincense spilling from his open chest. 'And Myrrh,' intoned the final magi.

"I understand gold and frankincense, but why myrrh?" I asked.

"It is a bit odd to give a spice used to anoint a body for burial. I asked the older magi about it later, 'we brought what we were impressed to bring,' was all I got out of him. Anyway," Levi said wanting to continue the story, "after the gifts were presented the magi bowed in worship.

'We are blessed by your gifts,' Joseph replied.

'We will treasure this moment and tell the child about it always,' added Mary.

'What have you named the child?' the older magi asked.

'Jesus,' the mother softly replied.

The magi conferred briefly, and then the old one spoke, 'I understand that, in your tongue, Jesus means God saves, it seems to fit the child.' With that, the magi rose, bowed once more, and proceeded from the room. The next morning they, the magi, and the young family were mysteriously all gone."

"Where did they go? I asked. "Did they leave a note or anything?"

"Both left a gold coin, well beyond what was owed. But I have no idea where they went." Levi answered.

"I know where," injected Dan. We both stared at him for a second.

"Go on, boy, you won't get in any trouble," assured

Levi.

"Joseph came to the stable early the next morning to get his donkey ready. He asked me to help him pack and that I was not to tell anyone. I asked him why they were leaving so suddenly. 'Do you believe in angels?' He asked. I nodded. 'One came to me in a dream and warned us to leave for Egypt because King Herod is going to try and kill Jesus. The angel also told me that the magi have also been warned in a dream not to return to Herod.'"

"Did Joseph say anything else?" I asked.

Dan thought for a moment, "Oh, yeah, I'm supposed to tell Levi something. 'Thank you for your hospitality, and the gold coin should cover our expenses. May God's blessings be with you.'"

I sat back to ponder Dan and Levi's story. Levi's right, I can't publish this until Herod is dead, it would be too dangerous. But, could this baby, this Jesus, be God's Messiah? That would be the scoop of the millennium. I made a mental note to ask a rabbi friend about the prophecies concerning the messiah when I returned home. Well, that leaves my angel sighting shepherd. "Dan, show me the donkey. I need to find a shepherd."

– Angels-

For two days, I bounced on the back of a donkey searching the Judean hill country for a specific shepherd named Samuel. I encountered several flocks along the way. All of them knew Judah's flock and Samuel, but none knew their location. I must have recrossed my path five or six times chasing down their suggestions. Near sunset, I crested a small hill. The lowering sun painted the clouds orange and purple in celebration of the waning day. In the darkening valley, I spotted another flock. With faltering hope of finding Samuel, I rode down to the nearest shepherd.

"Is this Judah's flock," I yelled when I got into range. The shepherd turned looking annoyed but waved me nearer.

"Don't yell like that," he hissed when I was close enough to hear, "we are getting the sheep settled for the night."

"Sorry is this Judah's flock or do you know where they might be?" I hissed back.

"This is Judah's flock. Is something wrong?" A worried look creasing the shepherd's eyes.

"No, nothing's wrong. I'm looking for Samuel."

"Do you see the man standing on the rock? That's Samuel." the shepherd said, pointing across the valley.

I could just make him out. "Thanks," I said, starting towards Samuel.

"Hey," the shepherd hissed again, "Don't go through the flock, go around." Changing direction, I again thanked the shepherd and rode on.

Darkness was complete long before I arrived at the rock. However, the shepherds had built a small cooking fire which helped to guide me in. Looking up, I marveled at the night sky. The brilliant stars reminded me of the magi, and I wondered what they saw that led them to Jesus. As I approached the fire, the one I took to be Samuel greeted me. "Good evening traveler, will you sup with us?" he asked, pointing at a spit of meat above the fire.

"Perhaps, I'm looking for Samuel."

"I am Samuel, do I know you?" the shepherd quizzed.

"Let's just say that we have a mutual friend. Do you remember the trader you ran into a week or so ago by a tent outside of Bethlehem."

The old shepherd thought for a moment, "you mean the night the child was born, the night the angels sang."

Bingo, I thought to myself, "yes, I'd like the hear your story, maybe do an article about it for the Jerusalem Journal."

"Sit traveler, I will never tire of telling about that night." Samuel looked at the other shepherds sitting around the fire. "We were all there, we all saw it." Samuel studied the stars for a moment. "It was just about this time. We had camped near Bethlehem to replenish our supplies." Samuel again stared into the night sky. "The stars were brilliant, just like tonight. Whenever they light the sky like this, I am reminded of God's promise to Abraham; that his descendants would be as numerous as the stars. I was pondering that promise when I saw one star seem to come closer and closer, growing in the night sky. Before I knew it, an angel was standing right in front of us. I fell to my knees, we all did."

"What did the angel look like?" I asked.

"He was taller than most men, bright, almost like looking into the sun. But it wasn't what I saw that frightened me, but what I felt. It was like being warmed by the sun but knowing that your heart was exposed before him. The angel must have sensed our fear because the first thing he said was, 'Do not be afraid!' That voice, deep and

163

powerful, for a moment I feared that it would cause the sheep to run, but they seemed unconcerned and calm. Then the angel said, 'I bring you good news that will bring great joy to all people. The Savior--yes, the Messiah, the Lord-- has been born today in Bethlehem, the city of David!' The Savior? The Messiah? In Bethlehem? What wonder is this, I thought. 'How shall we find the child?' I stammered. The angel explained, 'you will recognize him by this sign: You will find a baby wrapped snugly in strips of cloth, lying in a manger.' All of a sudden, the sky was filled with angels as if all the stars of heaven had come down to where we were at. With one voice they sang, 'Glory to God in highest heaven, and peace on earth to those with whom God is pleased!' They retreated back into the sky as their last note faded. We were all speechless. Finally, Joseph here exclaimed, 'Let's go to Bethlehem!' I agreed, 'let's see this thing that has happened which the Lord has told us about.' Without further discussion, we all ran to Bethlehem to search for the child.

At that moment, the fire crackled, throwing sparks into the air. I watched the sparks rise to join the stars and wondered what my reaction would have been. How marvelous and frightening to encounter those beings we call angels.

-The Search-

"How is the meat?" Samuel asked. During our meal, the other shepherds had shared their own experiences and feelings of that special night. I had a thousand questions. How many angels? Why announce to shepherds and magi, why not to the High Priest? Why is this baby special? You get the idea.

After they had all spoken, I told them about the magi's visit and the mysterious way they had been led to the baby. The shepherds enjoyed the news and wondered about the star. When I told them about the young family's hasty departure, they became worried and quiet. Desiring to keep the conversation going I asked, "can you tell me about your visit to the stable that night?"

Samuel straightened, his thoughts shifting from worry to his remembrance of that night. "We all ran towards Bethlehem, it was foolish and irresponsible to leave the flock like that."

"Your flock was watched while you were gone," I interrupted. "The trader outside of Bethlehem sent a servant to discover what caused you to run through his campsite. The servant found the flock unguarded and watched it until you returned."

"Praise God," Samuel rejoiced, "that is welcome news. Well, as you know, the younger ones of us ran ahead while I lagged behind. We were all excited and somewhat out of our heads with joy and wonder. But we managed to gather ourselves when we reached the outskirts of town. For a few moments, we debated how to proceed. It made sense for us to try the inn's stable first, it being the largest one in town. As we neared the stable, we spotted Dan the stable hand. I ran up to him and asked about the newborn.

'How do you know about...' he stammered.

'Where is he?' I demanded.

'In the rear stall,' he said, hurrying off.

Samuel looked at me and asked, "Do you go to the

Temple?"

"Yes, of course," I answered, surprised at the question's sudden shift.

"I always wondered what the priests felt when they entered the holy place, now I know. The stable was still a stable. The sights and smells were exactly the same. But the feeling, it was completely different. There was a quiet awe in that moment. I don't know how else to describe it." The other shepherds murmured their agreement.

"For me, it was like the deep watches of the night when everything is still, and God seems so close," added one shepherd.

"Thank you, Asher," nodded Samuel in agreement. "From the entrance, we could see the glow of a lamp near the rear of the cave. We quietly walked toward the light. The baby was lying in a manger lined with fresh straw, just like the angel had promised. The mother and father stood over the child, marveling at the new life before them. One of my shepherds knocked over a pot or something, alerting the mother and father to our presence. The father quickly positioned himself between the child and us."

'Why are you here?' he demanded.

Stepping forward, I meekly said, 'I am Samuel, we are shepherds, an angel told us that the Savior, the Messiah, is born this night and how to find him.' I knelt, and the others followed my lead. 'We have come to worship the gift God has given this evening.' The father glanced at the mother, who nodded in approval.

Stepping aside, the father said, 'I am Joseph of Nazareth, and this is my beloved Mary, the babe is called Jesus.'

'Please tell us more about the angel,' Mary asked. I recounted their appearance to her and repeated the angel's words. We continued to kneel before the babe, pondering the marvelous promises of God and worshipping Him. I didn't notice it, but soon I was the only shepherd left.

Standing, I said, 'the babe will need care like a young lamb. Keep watch over him, protect him, and keep him always close to his mother.'

'Thank you for all you have said,' Joseph responded.

'We will cherish it always,' Mary added.

With that, I bowed to each and slowly left them." There was silence around the campfire has the shepherds pondered their experience.

"Samuel," I said, breaking the silence, "who is this child, what is he to become?"

"I'm only a shepherd, not a rabbi, scribe, or priest. But, I have studied the scrolls. All of these events; the angels, the magi, and the baby, have reminded me of a passage from the prophet Isaiah. 'For a child is born to us, a son is given to us. The government will rest on his shoulders. And he will be called: Wonderful Counselor, Mighty God, Everlasting Father, Prince of Peace. His government and its peace will never end. He will rule with fairness and justice from the throne of his ancestor David for all eternity. The passionate commitment of the Lord of Heaven's Armies will make this happen!'"*

Somewhere in the flock, a lamb bleated for its mother. The fire crackled, a shepherd stirred, and a mama sheep softly replied. I slowly stood and wandered away from the shepherds, pondering all that I had heard. Staring into the night sky, I searched for a glimpse of whatever had led the magi or some residual trail of the angels. "You're looking in the wrong place for the answers you seek." A voice whispered. I turned, expecting, hoping that the voice was that of an angel. It was merely Samuel. "I, too, have pondered the stars, looking for some trace of God. Now I have seen angels. As marvelous and wonderful and frightening as that moment was they are simply messengers of God's grace."

"How do you know what I'm looking for?" I asked.

"Because it is common to all of us. We all seek some assurance that God is with us. I didn't understand it myself until I saw the babe. For years I had searched nature, searched scriptures, even searched other religions, but I gave up looking and became a simple shepherd. That night in the stable, I finally understood that I had only been seeking with my head. When I saw the babe, my heart was opened, changed in some way. Now everywhere I look, I see the hand of God. Did you see the sunset tonight? What did you think?"

"I thought it was beautiful," I said, recalling the vivid purples and oranges.

"A few weeks ago, I would have said the same thing. But tonight, as I stood on that rock taking it all in, I saw the handiwork of God, the brushstrokes of a master painter, a reminder of God's presence."

"All because you saw a baby?" I asked incredulously.

Samuel shook his head, "No, because I started looking with my heart. There is a promise in the law of Moses, one I had long overlooked. It goes, 'But from there(exile)you will search again for the Lord your God.

And if you search for him with all your heart and soul, you will find him.'** That night in the stable, I searched with my heart and found the Lord as the scripture promises. You too will find him if you search with all your heart. And when you find Jesus, you will find your answer." Samuel turned and walked away, leaving me with the stars and the sounds of the night.

*(Isaiah 9:6–7, NLT) **(Deuteronomy 4:29, NTL)

– Something is Changing –

Denny rolls the scroll and hands it back to me. "Nice story Squint, when are you going to publish it?"

"Not until it's safe for the child," I reply. For months I had watched for Denny's return to the market. I felt like I owed him the rest of the story. "So what do you think?"

"I don't know. Most folks think I'm this hard-nosed trader, always looking for a way to skin the other guy. But I spend a lot of time on the road, a lot of time thinking about life. I've come to agree with King Solomon – there's nothing new under the sun, all is vanity, a chasing after the wind. But this Bethlehem business doesn't seem to fit."

"That's a pretty brief summation of a whole book. You left out the part about there being a time for everything, perhaps this is a new time?" I suggest.

"I might disagree if I hadn't seen some of it with my own eyes. Angels, prophecies, magi. Something is changing." Denny responds.

"Something is changing, and it revolves around the

child born in the stable," I add.

"So Squint, did you publish anything from your trip to Bethlehem?"

"I did get one story, but I won't tell you unless you tell me something first."

"Okay, what is it?" Denny asks.

"Why do you call me Squint?"

"Oh, that's simple, you're always squinting around, looking into things. Like this baby thing, it started with a shepherd that knocked me over and muttered something about an angel. You look into it and discover not just a shepherd, but, a baby. And, not just a baby, but the long-promised Messiah that angels declared and magi sought out. So are you going to keep looking, keep squinting, for the child?"

"My editor isn't interested, so officially no. He says there are already too many stories about people claiming to be the messiah. I tried to remind him about the angels; he didn't buy it. It will probably be years from now, but, if the child is the Messiah of God, we won't be able to ignore him. And when he does show himself, I'll be there."

Denny nods in agreement, "so, what story did you publish?"

Putting on my best conspiratorial look, I reply, "The Injustice of Bribery, how some selfishly use their money and position."

"Sounds interesting, I could have given you all kinds of examples of how other merchants use bribery to get better prices."

"Well, I had a really good example. It seems that one trader tried to bribe an innkeeper in Bethlehem for a room, offering him three times the proper rate if he would kick out a family and give him the room."

"Ooh, you didn't?" Denny moans.

"I did," I affirmed, "but I left your name out of it."

ABOUT THE AUTHOR

Dale Heinold lives in rural Central Illinois with his wife Betty. They have two children and six grandchildren. Dale's primarily writes for Lambchow.com, but also works in IT as a system administrator. He can be contacted at dale@lambchow.com.

Made in the USA
Columbia, SC
08 September 2019